ANY GIVEN FATAL

AUSTRALIAN AMATEUR SLEUTH, BOOK 5

MORGANA BEST

Any Given Sundae
Australian Amateur Sleuth, Book 5
Copyright © 2016 by Morgana Best
All Rights Reserved
ISBN 9781925674231

No part of this book may be reproduced in any form or by any electronic or mechanical means, including information storage and retrieval systems, without written permission from the author, except for the use of brief quotations in a book review.

This is a work of fiction. Any resemblance to any person, living or dead, is purely coincidental. The personal names have been invented by the author, and any likeness to the name of any person, living or dead, is purely coincidental.

This book might contain references to specific commercial products, process or service by trade name, trademark, manufacturer, or otherwise, specific brand-name products and/or trade names of products, which are trademarks or registered trademarks and/or trade names, and these are property of their respective owners. Morgana Best or her associates have no association with any specific commercial products, process, or service by trade name, trademark, manufacturer, or otherwise, specific brand-name products and / or trade names of products.

GLOSSARY

Some Australian spellings and expressions are entirely different from US spellings and expressions. Below are just a few examples.

It would take an entire book to list all the differences.

For example, people often think "How are you going?" (instead of "How are you doing?") is an error, but it's normal and correct for Aussies!

The author has used Australian spelling in this series. Here are a few examples: *Mum* instead of the US spelling *Mom, neighbour* instead of the US spelling *neighbor, realise* instead of the US spelling *realize*. It is *Ms, Mr* and *Mrs* in Australia, not *Ms., Mr.* and *Mrs.*; *defence* not *defense; judgement* not *judg-*

ment; cosy and not *cozy; 1930s* not *1930's; offence* not *offense; centre* not *center; towards* not *toward; jewellery* not *jewelry; favour* not *favor; mould* not *mold; two storey house* not *two story house; practise* (verb) not *practice* (verb); *odour* not *odor; smelt* not *smelled; travelling* not *traveling; liquorice* not *licorice; cheque not check; leant* not *leaned; have concussion* not *have a concussion; anti clockwise* not *counterclockwise; go to hospital* not *go to the hospital; sceptic* not *skeptic; aluminium* not *aluminum; learnt* not *learned*. We have *fancy dress* parties not *costume* parties. We don't say *gotten*. We say *car crash* (or *accident*) not *car wreck*. We say *a herb* not *an herb* as we pronounce the 'h.'

The above are just a few examples.

It's not just different words; Aussies sometimes use different expressions in sentence structure. We might *eat a curry* not *eat curry*. We might say *in the main street* not *on the main street*. Someone might be *going well* instead of *doing well*. We might say *without drawing breath* not *without drawing a breath*.

These are just some of the differences.

Please note that these are not mistakes or typos, but correct, normal Aussie spelling, terms, and syntax.

AUSTRALIAN SLANG AND TERMS

Benchtops - counter tops (kitchen)
Big Smoke - a city
Blighter - infuriating or good-for-nothing person
Blimey! - an expression of surprise
Bloke - a man (usually used in nice sense, "a good bloke")
Blue (noun) - an argument ("to have a blue")
Bluestone - copper sulphate (copper sulfate in US spelling)
Bluo - a blue laundry additive, an optical brightener
Boot (car) - trunk (car)
Bonnet (car) - hood (car)
Bore - a drilled water well
Budgie smugglers (variant: budgy smugglers) - named after the Aussie native bird, the budgerigar. A slang term for brief and tight-fitting men's swimwear
Bugger! - as an expression of surprise, not a swear word
Bugger - as in "the poor bugger" - refers to an unfortunate person (not a swear word)
Bunging it on - faking something, pretending

Bush telegraph - the grapevine, the way news spreads by word of mouth in the country
Car park - parking lot
Cark it - die
Chooks - chickens
Come good - turn out okay
Copper, cop - police officer
Coot - silly or annoying person
Cream bun - a sweet bread roll with copious amounts of cream, plus jam (= jelly in US) in the centre
Crook - 1. "Go crook (on someone)" - to berate them. 2. (someone is) crook - (someone is) ill. 3. Crook (noun) - a criminal
Demister (in car) - defroster
Drongo - an idiot
Dunny - an outhouse, a toilet, often ramshackle
Fair crack of the whip - a request to be fair, reasonable, just
Flannelette (fabric) - cotton, wool, or synthetic fabric, one side of which has a soft finish.
Flat out like a lizard drinking water - very busy
Galah - an idiot
Garbage - trash
G'day - Hello
Give a lift (to someone) - give a ride (to someone)

Goosebumps - goose pimples
Gumboots - rubber boots, wellingtons
Knickers - women's underwear
Laundry (referring to the room) - laundry room
Lamingtons - iconic Aussie cakes, square, sponge, chocolate-dipped, and coated with desiccated coconut. Some have a layer of cream and strawberry jam (= jelly in US) between the two halves.
Lift - elevator
Like a stunned mullet - very surprised
Mad as a cut snake - either insane or very angry
Mallee bull (as fit as, as mad as) - angry and/or fit, robust, super strong.
Miles - while Australians have kilometres these days, it is common to use expressions such as, "The road stretched for miles," "It was miles away."
Moleskins - woven heavy cotton fabric with suede-like finish, commonly used as working wear, or as town clothes
Mow (grass / lawn) - cut (grass / lawn)
Neenish tarts - Aussie tart. Pastry base. Filling is based on sweetened condensed milk mixture or mock cream. Some have layer of raspberry jam (jam = jelly in US). Topping is in two equal halves: icing (= frosting in US), usually chocolate

on one side, and either lemon or pink on the other.

Pub - The pub at the south of a small town is often referred to as the 'bottom pub' and the pub at the north end of town, the 'top pub.' The size of a small town is often judged by the number of pubs - i.e. "It's a three pub town."

Red cattle dog - (variant: blue cattle dog usually known as a 'blue dog') - referring to the breed of Australian Cattle Dog. However, a 'red dog' is usually a red kelpie (another breed of dog)

Shoot through - leave

Shout (a drink) - to buy a drink for someone

Skull (a drink) - drink a whole drink without stopping

Stone the crows! - an expression of surprise

Takeaway (food) - Take Out (food)

Toilet - also refers to the room if it is separate from the bathroom

Torch - flashlight

Tuck in (to food) - to eat food hungrily

Ute /Utility - pickup truck

Vegemite - Australian food spread, thick, dark brown

Wardrobe - closet

Windscreen - windshield

Indigenous References

Bush tucker - food that occurs in the Australian bush

Koori - the original inhabitants/traditional custodians of the land of Australia in the part of NSW in which this book is set. *Murri* are the people just to the north. White European culture often uses the term, *Aboriginal people.*

CHAPTER 1

I shuddered against the icy wind and closed the window as quickly as I could, sighing with relief as it slammed shut. It was the middle of winter here in Little Tatterford, a place where it got cold enough for water pipes to freeze solid. In other words, it was the sort of town in which going outside was entirely too much trouble for a full quarter of each year. Sure, it got colder in other parts of the world, but for some reason, Australian houses were not built for this climate. Perhaps it had something to do with the fact that the rest of Australia was either desert or nice, warm, and coastal.

I looked out of the window, struggling to see much through the fog that was rapidly building against the glass. All the trees had long since shed their leaves, leaving nothing but depressing grey-brown skeletons jutting out of the ground at strange angles, making the entire horizon infinitely more ominous. The sky was similarly devoid of colour as clouds gathered, and although the chance of actual snow was currently next to zero, there was always the possibility of a hailstorm. The last one had been some time ago, but had been serious enough to litter the ground in hail and cause considerable damage to houses and cars. Nobody was happy to take a day off work because it was hailing so heavily.

I sighed again and turned away from the window, narrowly dodging an antique chair nearby. The boarding house was filled to the brim with antiques of every sort, but furniture was the worst offender. There were more chairs than there had ever been guests, and not nearly enough tables to seat them all. Each chair was drastically different from the others, a bizarre ensemble of antiques that looked as though it was specifically a collection from different periods of history.

Happily, each was clean, practically shining in the electric light cast down from the high ceilings. That was due to one Mr Buttons, the only permanent boarder and a man who spent far too much time cleaning. He had been a good friend of mine since I'd moved to Little Tatterford after a nasty divorce, and was best described as a typical English butler, though he never did any actual butlering. He spent his free time cleaning things, whether or not it was socially acceptable to do so, and making cucumber sandwiches with the crusts cut off, though he'd recently tried branching out into more exciting recipes, such as watercress sandwiches—with the crusts cut off.

I looked around the boarding house, taking in the bizarre sights. I'd gotten so used to being here that I sometimes forgot what a strange place it really was. Other than the scattering of antiques, the house was a grand Victorian affair with high ceilings, striking arches, and a grand staircase. It was a beautiful building, though it did feel somewhat out of place in a small Australian country town. I considered that it wasn't built for such cold weather, as I pulled my jacket tightly around myself and shivered.

I grimaced as I noticed several large hairs on my jacket. I quickly brushed them off. Since moving to Little Tatterford, I'd started my own dog and cat grooming business and had struggled to get it up and running. More recently, though, I'd become quite successful with it, though it did mean occasionally finding about four pets' worth of hair on my person. I knew if I myself didn't brush it off, then Mr Buttons wouldn't be able to help himself. He was very nice and a good friend, but his obsession with cleanliness extended far beyond social normality.

"Sibyl!" A familiar voice called out my name. I turned to see Mr Buttons walking briskly towards me, Cressida in tow. Cressida was the owner of the boarding house and also a good friend of mine, yet it was hard to talk about her without mentioning how, well, unique she was. She wore altogether too much make-up, as though she were trying to blend into the background of a clown painting.

Speaking of painting, that was her hobby of choice. Unfortunately, her subject of choice was disturbingly gory settings, making her nevertheless skilled artworks somewhat hard to look at.

"Hello, Mr Buttons. Hi, Cressida," I said with a smile.

"I didn't think you'd be here so early," Cressida said, dusting herself off. Mr Buttons raised an eyebrow and looked at her, clearly sizing her up for a cleaning. Cressida seemed to notice and took a step away from him.

"Sorry, it's just so hard to sit still in the cold like this, so I decided to get here a bit earlier than we'd agreed," I explained. I lived in a cottage not too far from the boarding house, and while it was better insulated than the boarding house itself, it was still impossible to stay warm in this weather. I'd figured that a walk would do me some good, but had underestimated just how cold it was outside.

We all walked to the dining room together where Mr Buttons made us some tea. I thanked him and took a slow sip, enjoying the heat as much as possible. The tea was good, but I was more interested in garnering every bit of warmth that I could.

"So I hear your business is taking off," Mr Buttons said with a smile.

"You could say that," I said. "I've been doing very well lately, yes. It seems that a lot of people have been moving here from Sydney, probably looking for a more rural lifestyle. My client base has increased recently, and while the work has been nothing short of exhausting, I'm glad for it," I admitted. It had been hard trying to make a living when my business was struggling so much previously, so it was a relief to have such a reliable income.

"Would you like some lunch?" Cressida suddenly interjected. "Dorothy is in, so she should..."

"No!" a voice yelled from the kitchen nearby. "I'm not in the mood," the voice continued. I sighed, recognising Dorothy's voice at once. She was a large unpleasant woman, the relatively recent cook of the boarding house. Ever since she had taken the job, the quality of food had decreased dramatically, and she was nothing short of rude to everybody in conversation. Mr Buttons especially held disdain for her, though he expressed it in his own strange way.

"Cease and desist, madam!" Mr Buttons yelled back. "We are your guests, and you should feel honour-bound to meet our needs!" He said it with so much confidence that I was sure he himself believed it. Dorothy responded with a noise somewhere between a furious "Humph!" and the sound of a pig being squeezed. Mr Buttons took what could only be explained as an angry sip of tea and set his cup back down delicately on the saucer, looking perturbed. I held in a laugh. While I wasn't exactly the biggest fan of Dorothy, it was always fun to watch how Mr Buttons struggled against her tyranny.

"And what else is new, Sibyl?" Cressida asked, obviously hoping to change the topic of conversation.

"Well, the property settlement with my ex-husband has been awarded," I announced cheerfully. "I'm just waiting for the money to come through."

"And how is all that... unpleasantness affecting you?" Mr Buttons asked.

I at once knew what he meant. "As you know, they've both been convicted of murder." I let out a long sigh of relief. My ex-husband and his mistress had tried to murder me some time ago. They had received a long term prison sentence both for my attempted murder and for the murder of someone else, so it was unlikely that I'd have to worry about them for a long time.

"That's excellent!" Cressida exclaimed. "Well, not excellent as such, I suppose. But it's good for you," she added with a weak smile.

I laughed before replying. "It's fine, Cressida. We weren't exactly friends before he tried to murder me, so there's no love lost, so to speak." I looked at Mr Buttons, who was apparently still concentrating on his distaste for Dorothy. Talking to Cressida seemed like the best option when Mr Buttons was in this kind of mood. "And how are things with you, Cressida?" I asked.

"Great!" she announced excitedly. "Five of my paintings have sold from Mortimer's gallery already."

I gasped, although managed to hide my shock by pretending it was a delighted sort of noise. I was happy for her, but it amazed me that people were willing to buy her art when everything she depicted was so gruesome and graphic. I couldn't remember the last time I saw one of her paintings without immediately feeling the kind of existential dread typically reserved by the highest order of horror fiction.

She'd recently sold some pieces to an art dealer by the name of Mortimer Fyfe-Waring, who was every bit as strange as his name suggested. He was an older man, about her age, who ran a gallery in a nearby town. He had become inconsolably excited when he had seen her artworks and had commissioned them on the spot. At first, I thought he was just crazy, but then I figured he was probably good at his job—and crazy. The fact that the paintings were selling so quickly told me that I probably didn't have an eye for art, and that I certainly didn't want one.

"He's also asked me to paint some more, since the last ones sold so quickly," Cressida said happily. Before I could escape, she pulled a canvas from seemingly nowhere and showed me. I resisted the urge to scream, though barely, and managed to nod approvingly, making the most positive noise I could through gritted teeth. "This is part of a new collection I call *The Obliteration of Newbury*," Cressida explained kindly. I didn't think to ask what she had against Newbury or happiness, instead focusing on changing the topic immediately. Unfortunately, she maintained a level stare as if waiting for some kind of response.

"It sure is something," I said, trying to smile.

"Oh, I can't wait to show Mortimer," Cressida said with a genuine smile.

"I'm not sure what you see in him," Mr Buttons butted in, apparently part of the conversation again. "I find him rather off-putting," he continued, clearing his throat.

"Oh, pish posh," Cressida said. "He's a nice man. It's good to meet someone normal," she continued, apparently completely oblivious to the notion of irony.

"He *is* gay, you know," Mr Buttons said, sipping his tea.

"He is not always!" Cressida exclaimed. "Sometimes he's quite sad."

"What about that Vlad he's always talking about?" Mr Buttons asked.

"They're just friends who sometimes massage each other in the sauna," Cressida explained as though it were normal. "He told me all this when we met for lunch," she said smugly.

"Anyway," I interjected, hoping to change the topic before it got even stranger and more awkward. "What else is new, Cressida? How has business at the boarding house been?"

"Oh, not bad, not bad. Lord Farringdon has warned me that there's an enemy closer to us than we realise, though," she said casually, taking another sip of tea. Lord Farringdon was her cat, and of course Cressida thought she could communicate with him. It was easy to dismiss her as a crazy cat lady, but Lord Farringdon had made an alarming number of accurate predictions. I took a moment to consider that a single accurate prediction from an allegedly talking cat was an alarming number, but decided to focus on the topic at hand.

"What does that mean?" I asked.

"He said that something horrible will happen soon," she said, setting down her tea cup. "Something bad and something near." Cressida leant in close to me and lowered her voice to a whisper. "But the most important thing to remember is that he's a bit paranoid, you know, that one. He's getting on in years." She leant back and nodded at me knowingly.

I sighed, feeling altogether less calm than I had been before. We'd had our share of problems here in Little Tatterford, and I hoped that the prophetic cat was just a product of Cressida's imagination.

CHAPTER 2

I immediately regretted not choosing a warmer jacket. The air was bitterly cold, and I hugged myself tightly to try to garner some warmth. I considered running back to the cottage to get something more appropriate for the temperature, but figured it would probably be quicker to get inside the boarding house. I was more than halfway there and decided to run the rest of the way, awkwardly trying to keep my footing on the frosty ground as my crossed arms provided nothing in the way of balance.

I finally arrived at the front door, having nearly fallen over several times. It was raining lightly, and the little bits of sleet caused me to shiver with every drop that hit me. I looked up at the sky. It was already pitch black, despite the sun not having set quite yet. I knew it was close to setting, but the pitch-black clouds stopped me telling exactly what time it was. It looked like a huge storm was coming and I knew I'd want to be back in my cottage before it hit. I considered leaving immediately, but thought the better of it.

I had agreed to come around for dinner when Cressida had asked me. There were new boarders she wanted me to meet, though I wasn't thrilled about the idea. It seemed like every time I met boarders it ended in disaster, and what Lord Farringdon, or rather, what Cressida had said earlier, had put me on edge ever since. *Something bad is coming.* I looked up at the storm, shivered, swallowed hard, and pushed my way through the front door and into the boarding house.

"Sibyl!" Cressida called out immediately. I barely had a chance to acknowledge her before she hugged me tightly. "Thanks for coming. Everybody's already sitting around for dinner, so let's go." She led me into the dining room before I could so much as speak.

The dining room was well-lit and much warmer than I had anticipated, making me happy about my choice of apparel for the first time this winter. Mr Buttons was sitting at the table next to a man I didn't recognise, who in turn was sitting next to another woman who likewise was a stranger to me. Opposite him sat another woman who seemed to be slightly younger than either of the others. Cressida sat at the head of the table and I took a seat opposite Mr Buttons, next to the youngest of the new trio.

"Ah, hello, Sibyl," Mr Buttons said with a smile. "These are the new boarders." He motioned to the three who all smiled at me.

The woman who was sitting beside me spoke. "I'm Prudence Paget." She extended a hand. I took it and shook it, smiling back.

"I'm Sally," said the woman who was furthest away in a meek tone. She didn't make eye contact, and I considered that maybe she was just shy.

"I'm Dr. Roland Cavendish," the last stranger, the man, said. "You may call me Roland." He took my hand and kissed the back of it. I withdrew my hand quickly, looking to Mr Buttons for an explanation. He simply shrugged slightly, looking nearly as confused as I felt. I considered that maybe Roland was just being polite in his own creepy way, but there was undoubtedly something unsettling about him. I thought back to Lord Farringdon's warning and shuddered.

"Uh, nice to meet you all," I stammered. "I'm Sibyl. I live in the cottage down the road. You might have noticed it."

"Oh, yes, it looks cute!" Prudence exclaimed. "I mean, from the outside. I didn't get a very good look either, if I'm honest, but from what I could tell it seems like a nice place. Do you mind if I ask what it is you do? As a job, I mean."

"Oh," I cleared my throat. "I'm a pet groomer. Dogs and cats, specifically. Business has been good here in Little Tatterford, despite what some people assume," I said with a chuckle. "Small town and all that. What about you?" I asked Prudence, noticing that the others had started their own conversations.

"Academia. I'm actually here to give a public paper on the Spotted Quoll at the university. The quoll is a little carnivorous marsupial, in case you were wondering." She laughed. "The number two question I'm asked is, 'What exactly is a quoll?'"

"What is the number one question?" I asked.

She laughed again. "Why quolls?"

I smiled, but stopped when I noticed Sally was still looking sadly down at the table. I thought that maybe she was shy and that talking to her might just make her even more uncomfortable, but thought I might as well. "What do you do, Sally?" I asked politely. She looked up at me with a shocked expression and took a moment to compose herself before replying.

"She's my wife," Roland replied, as though that were an answer to my question. Sally looked sadly down at the table again and sighed softly. "I'm a noted quantum physicist," Roland announced proudly, going so far as to puff out his chest as he spoke. "I've taken up a post as a Visiting Fellow at the university in Pharmidale." He smiled lasciviously at me the entire time he spoke, and I felt immediately repulsed by him. Sally was still looking sad, though I considered that she looked a lot happier than I would if I had to be married to Roland. I noticed that Prudence was hanging off every word he said, with a huge smile plastered across her face. Cressida was listening politely, and Mr Buttons seemed to be rubbing at a tiny smear on Roland's jacket, much to Roland's confused embarrassment.

"I see," I replied coolly. I didn't know Roland very well, but I'd already decided not to like him.

Prudence and Roland appeared to be flirting

shamelessly with one another as the night dragged on, much to Sally's ire. I tried in vain to cheer her up, but it was clear that she didn't want to talk. The awkwardness was broken by the unlikeliest hero as Dorothy burst into the room brandishing a serving spoon.

"I heard you complaining about the food!" she yelled, pointing the serving spoon at Mr Buttons as though it were a gun.

"I didn't complain about a thing, you great oaf," Mr Buttons retaliated as he stood. "You just want to start some drama," he continued.

Dorothy turned around, I assume to accuse others, when a horrified look crossed her face, as though Mr Buttons had accused her of killing more than just the meal. She clearly then decided that the best course of action was to scream every profanity imaginable, as well as some I'm sure must have been invented on the spot.

Roland butted in. "You look familiar," he began, "although the person I had you confused with was much younger. Still, it was years ago." Dorothy glared at him, but he continued. "I'm sure the food is wonderful, but I have a rare condition known as hypogeusia. It means I have a decreased ability to taste food. It's a congenital thing."

As Roland's voice droned on with mention of T2R taste receptor genes in his tongue and other less than gripping facts, Dorothy and Mr Buttons faced off.

"All right, that's enough!" Cressida snapped. She jumped to her feet. "You two need to stop fighting, because you're both here to stay. So get used to each other, because there are no other options, and it's upsetting Lord Farringdon."

Mr Buttons sighed and sat back down, and Dorothy just marched back out of the room in a huff. Sally watched her leave with a confused expression on her face, and I noticed that Roland and Prudence were looking intently at one another.

Eventually, the guests left for their rooms one by one. Roland and Sally were the exception, leaving together, though Prudence followed closely behind.

"I don't like that Roland," I admitted to Cressida and Mr Buttons as we walked to the front door.

"Why ever not?" Cressida asked. "He seemed nice enough to me."

"No, he was flirting with Prudence—and with me too, for that matter. It was creepy! His poor wife, Sally, looked so upset," I explained. Mr Buttons nodded sullenly.

"Oh, he wasn't flirting," Cressida said, smiling. "He's just like that."

"A notorious flirt?" I asked. I wasn't at all surprised that Cressida hadn't noticed, but I was still annoyed by it.

"They have already had quite a loud fight," Cressida added.

I was confused. "Who?"

"Why, Roland and Sally, of course." Cressida leant down to stroke Lord Farringdon. "They had an awful row just after they checked in."

"Come on, Sibyl, it's time to go," Mr Buttons said calmly. "I think it's been a strange night for all of us. I'll see you tomorrow for our walk?" he asked, raising an eyebrow. I agreed.

I walked back to my cabin alone, hugging my jacket tightly against the icy wind. I couldn't stop thinking about poor Sally. Her marriage reminded me of my own, but at least I was well out of it now. I hurried on to my cottage, the warmth of my fire beckoning me.

CHAPTER 3

"Wonderful day, isn't it?" Mr Buttons asked happily. I considered that I should slap him, or perhaps have him assessed by a professional. Mr Buttons and I were walking through the freezing cold morning frost with Sandy in tow. It couldn't quite decide whether to rain or snow, so light falls of both alternated. How anybody could consider this 'wonderful' was utterly beyond me. I shivered violently and considered sprinting back to my cabin, but didn't want to leave Sandy behind. Plus, I wasn't sure if my muscles would work quite right in this kind of weather.

"What do you think of the new boarders?" I asked, desperate to take my mind off the cold.

"I agree with you about Roland," Mr Buttons said sadly. "I don't think that's a marriage that will last. Excuse me for saying so, but I hope it doesn't. Poor Sally seems like she deserves better. I heard them screaming at each other last night about his mistress."

I tried to stop my teeth chattering long enough to speak. "She accused him of having a mistress?"

Mr Buttons shook his head. "No, poor Sally already knows about his mistress. From what I heard, he has insisted on having an open marriage for some time, but Sally doesn't want that. He told her that his mistress was coming to town soon and that Sally would have to face facts."

"Poor Sally! Actually, I called her last night to invite her over for an ice cream sundae this morning. I felt like she could use a friend here," I explained, smiling. I'd called her right after dinner the previous night, and she had answered at once. She sounded friendly enough, if a little distracted. I figured that Dorothy had said something to upset her, as I'd called the front desk, had the misfortune to speak to Dorothy, and had asked to be put through to Sally's room.

"Sibyl, that's very nice of you, but have you considered that an ice cream sundae might not be the best idea in this kind of weather?" Mr Buttons gestured to the frost all around us as Sandy found a heavy patch to roll in.

I felt myself blushing a little. "I actually hadn't considered that," I admitted. "But I could add hot fudge, and we can have a hot chocolate with it, or something." I shrugged. "Honestly, it was just a way to talk to Sally in private, or at least without Roland there. I don't mean to be snooping so much, but something about their relationship seemed off, something apart from Roland's shameless flirting. It reminded me of my own marriage. I just want to make sure she's okay." I sighed and then watched as my breath turned to ice.

"I understand, Sibyl," Mr Buttons said warmly. "Now we should be heading back before you freeze entirely. You don't seem to be handling the cold quite as well as I thought you would by now," he teased.

"I don't think anybody could be handling this cold," I said through chattering teeth. "I couldn't have a hot shower this morning because the pipes had frozen solid. That's not okay!"

I put Sandy's leash on her and we walked back to the boarding house, far too slowly for my liking. Mr Buttons was enjoying the walk nearly as much as Sandy was, but I couldn't wait to be back inside where it was warmer. I considered that maybe I should call off the meeting with Sally and instead book a meeting with my bed and a hot water bottle, but decided that talking to her would be for the best.

Mr Buttons and I said our goodbyes as he stepped back into the boarding house, and Sandy and I continued on to the cottage. As we approached the cottage, Sandy barked furiously, tearing free from my grasp and hurtling towards the door. She scratched at the door and continued barking loudly. My heart froze in my chest.

I seized Sandy's leash and held it tightly, making sure she wouldn't run at anybody in the house unless I wanted her to. I pushed the door and it swung open. It had been unlocked—this was the country, after all. No one locked their cars or houses around here. I swallowed nervously and entered.

"Hello?" I called out. I figured that if someone was here to hurt me, they'd already have heard me enter, and anybody else would just respond. Unfortunately, there was no response. I crept forward slowly, struggling against Sandy who was pulling hard on her leash. I turned into the kitchen and gasped.

There, on my cottage floor, lay Roland Cavendish. He was dead.

Next to him sat a half-eaten ice cream sundae.

CHAPTER 4

"Sorry, Sibyl, but it'll take some time," Blake explained apologetically. "We have to sweep your house for evidence and obviously move the body, but it shouldn't take more than a day. In the meantime, can you stay there?" He motioned to the boarding house. We were standing outside the boarding house's entrance as several police officers explored the inside of my cottage. I was too in shock to feel anything but the biting cold.

"It should be fine," I said weakly.

"We'll also have to ask you and the boarders some questions, of course," Blake said with a sigh. "It was definitely poison, given his symptoms. Sibyl, how are you holding up?"

"Better than most, I suppose," I said. "I mean, I'm not exactly used to this sort of thing, despite how much it's happened. But I'll be okay, Blake, really. Thanks for asking." I shot him the best smile I could, but didn't maintain it for long. I sat on the front steps of the boarding house with a small sigh. "Do you know what killed him?"

Blake shook his head. "Only that it was poison. Well, I'll be back with Constable Andrews to ask everyone some questions, you included. Sorry to do it, but we don't really have a choice, given the circumstances," he admitted.

"It's fine, I understand." I smiled again. Blake smiled back and walked in the direction of my cottage. I hugged my knees for warmth.

"Come inside, Sibyl. I'll make you some tea," Cressida said from behind me. I looked over my shoulder and nodded at her before following her inside.

We were soon sitting in the dining room in front of a roaring fire. I nursed my tea in my hands, enjoying the heat.

"Can you tell me exactly what happened?" Cressida asked. "I don't mean to pry and I understand if you can't talk about it, but I want to know what happened. All I know is that Roland was found dead," she said sadly.

Before I could reply, Mr Buttons burst into the room. "Sibyl! Are you okay? What happened?"

"I'm okay. Well, I'm not hurt, at least," I said, cupping my head in my hands. "I found Roland dead in my home."

"I heard that much," Mr Buttons said, taking a seat next to me. "Are you able to talk about what happened?"

"We were in the middle of that!" Cressida said.

"After our walk, I went straight home. Sandy was barking, and I thought that maybe there was an intruder in the house. I went inside to find Roland lying on the ground next to an ice cream sundae," I explained, though I wasn't sure if it made any more sense to them than it did to me. "He'd eaten most of it, and Blake said he'd been poisoned. I'm sure the detectives will suspect me."

Cressida raised her eyebrows. "An ice cream sundae?"

"Yes. What's worse is that I'd invited Sally over later to have an ice cream sundae, though she wasn't even meant to be there yet. I hadn't even prepared the sundae, so it's all quite a mystery. I'm not sure if the police know where Sally is." I sighed again.

"I think she's still in her room," Cressida said. "The police went up there to deliver the news and I haven't seen them in a bit. I imagine if she wasn't there then they'd be back by now."

"Oh, I hope she's okay," I said, as a wave of sadness washed over me. Roland and Sally didn't seem like they were getting along so smoothly, but it would still be a horrible thing to lose one's husband like that. At least, that's assuming that she wasn't the killer. A chill ran up my spine as I considered the thought. She seemed a likely suspect, but it was far too early to know.

"The police want to question all of us later on," I told them, though neither seemed surprised. "It's Blake and Constable Andrews, so it'll be friendly, at least." I'd much rather be doing anything than being questioned about this, especially when I knew so little, but I also didn't want to go home. Not for a long time, at least. All I could think of was Roland, just lying there. What had happened? Why was he even at my cottage? Who would want to poison him?

"Let either of us know if we can do

anything to help, dear," Cressida said, forcing a smile. "I'm sure it'll all work itself out," she continued in a less than convincing tone, though I appreciated the attempt to make me feel better.

Mr Buttons, Cressida, and I sat in silence for at least another hour, though it might have been more, before Blake and Constable Andrews came to question us.

"All right, we'll need to talk to all of you and ask you some questions. Cressida, could you please gather all the boarders and take them into the front room? Mr Buttons, I'm afraid I'll have to ask you to follow her while Andrews and I question Sibyl," Blake explained calmly. Cressida and Mr Buttons nodded before heading off, and Blake and Constable Andrews sat opposite me at the dining table.

"Sorry about this, Sibyl." Blake's tone was earnest. "I'd love it if we could hold off or just not do this questioning thing at all, but it's important that we do."

"I understand, don't worry," I said calmly. "Ask away. I'm afraid I probably won't be too much help, though."

"Just try your best," Andrews said.

"Sibyl, how did you discover the body?" Blake asked.

I had already explained this when I'd called him, but figured it was more of a formality than anything. "I came home from a walk with Mr Buttons. We were out walking Sandy..."

"Sandy being your dog?" Andrews asked.

"Yes, that's right," I said, nodding. "Anyway, I walked back here with Mr Buttons and then went straight home. Sandy was barking at the door when I got close, and I thought that maybe someone was inside. I called out but didn't hear anything, and then I went in and saw Roland lying on the floor."

"Was the sundae there when you arrived?" Blake asked.

"Yes, it was," I said. "I'd invited his wife Sally over for an ice cream sundae later today, but I haven't seen her at all since last night. I imagine it's all related, though," I admitted. I didn't want to place blame on Sally just because of the circumstances, but I trusted Blake not to jump to any conclusions.

"Why did you invite her over?" Andrews asked.

I swallowed nervously before answering.

"Well, because she seemed to be fighting with Roland at dinner last night." I realised my answers were clearly implicating her, but then again maybe she really had killed Roland. "She seemed somehow sad or distant all throughout dinner. Honestly, I only met her last night, so I don't know if that's even out of character, but I thought I'd try to cheer her up a bit."

Andrews looked up from his notes. "Who knew you had invited her?"

I shrugged. "I have no idea. I mean, Dorothy answered the front desk phone and I asked to be put through to Sally, so Dorothy could've listened in. And I suppose Roland knew, too."

Blake smiled at me as I explained it all, though Andrews kept a neutral expression. It seemed more and more obvious to me that Sally might have had a hand in what happened.

"Can you tell us more about what happened last night?" Blake asked as Andrews scribbled something in his notebook.

"Well, not much, to tell the truth," I said simply.

"Every little bit could help. Try not to miss any details," Andrews said without looking up from whatever he was writing.

I took a deep breath and spoke. "Well, we were all having dinner to greet the new boarders. There was myself, Mr Buttons, Cressida, Roland and Sally Cavendish, and Prudence Paget. Oh, and Dorothy, who was cooking. It was an uneventful night, more or less. I noticed that Roland was flirting with Prudence, despite being married to Sally. He tried flirting with me, too," I added, noticing that Blake's eye twitched as I mentioned it, "though of course, I didn't respond. Prudence, on the other hand, was happily flirting back."

"Did anything else happen? Anything at all?" Andrews pressed.

"Not that I can think of," I admitted. "Oh, well, Dorothy and Mr Buttons had a bit of an argument, but that almost goes without saying nowadays."

"What was it over?" Blake asked.

"I don't know, really. Dorothy came in screaming that Mr Buttons was complaining about her food, though he hadn't been. Dorothy's just like that, I suppose. I can't imagine what this has to do with Roland, though. Roland, Sally, and Prudence weren't involved in the argument at all," I explained with a shrug. "Oh, and Roland said he had a genetic condition that means he can't taste food. I can't remember the name of it."

"Thanks, Sibyl," Blake said warmly. "You've been a big help. Now I'm going to call in the others one at a time. Would you ask Cressida to come in, please?"

As I left the room, it dawned on me that I might seriously be a suspect in the case, given that a man had been murdered in my home. I opened the door into a solid object, and saw Mr Buttons and Cressida there, listening in. They signalled to me to remain silent. I nodded, and whispered to Cressida that she was to go in next.

As soon as she was through the door, Mr Buttons and I put our ears to the door, while Lord Farringdon meowed loudly and scratched at the door. It was hard to listen at the same time as trying to stop Lord Farringdon giving the game away. Finally, Mr Buttons stroked Lord Farringdon while I listened. Cressida spent her time stressing that the murder technically occurred outside of the boarding house, and that if and when the media caught wind of it, then the police should emphasise that fact. Blake tried his best to explain that he had very little control over the media, but Cressida just kept insisting until eventually Blake agreed to do his best.

It was all Cressida and I could do not to laugh when it was Mr Buttons' turn to be questioned. In typical form, he spent most of his interview telling Constable Andrews that he needed to scrub a small stain out of the table. They'd eventually managed to ask him all the usual questions, and his story matched up with mine, as was to be expected.

Blake and Andrews interviewed Dorothy next, though she was her usual unhelpful self. All she did throughout the interview was complain about their manners and the state of the boarding house, and eventually Blake let her go with a frustrated sigh. She marched out of the room and announced that we were to fetch Prudence Paget for questioning, and that she was going to guard the door to make sure that no one listened in. She crossed her arms over her ample bosom as she said it. I led Mr Buttons away before he managed to reply.

"Mr Buttons," I said as we reached the dining room and I stood with my back to the fire, "Blake will have to call in the detectives, and I'm sure they'll suspect me." I hoped Mr Buttons would disagree.

"I'm afraid you're right, Sibyl," he said solemnly. "A man appeared in your house and died after eating a sundae, so they will no doubt assume it *is* suspicious."

CHAPTER 5

"Thank you so much!" The woman beamed as she took her Bernese Mountain Dog out of the grooming tent while he desperately tried to sniff something nearby. I laughed as he shot me a look that could only be described as goofy before disappearing from sight.

I sighed, sitting down in my chair and leaning back. It had been a long day, though a lucrative one. I was at the Pharmidale Dog Show, grooming show dogs before they went and had their day in the sun, so to speak. The best part about working at a dog show—other than the pay—was that the dogs were generally much better behaved. The humans weren't, necessarily, but at least most of them had been friendly. I guessed that some of them were simply succumbing to stress, and having a stranger groom their dog probably added to that. Otherwise, a small percentage of them seemed to be natural-born jerks.

The major events were beginning, so I suspected I'd have a bit of a break before another onslaught of customers. I appreciated all the work, but I appreciated the rest a whole lot more.

To my surprise, two men walked into my tent. My heart sank as I recognised Detective Roberts. He was with Blake, which made me feel a little better, but I doubted they'd come to watch me work.

"What do you want?" I asked, cutting straight to the point. Today wasn't the time to beat around the bush.

"We need you to come down to the station with us," Blake said seriously, wearing the grimmest expression I had seen on him. He shifted uncomfortably as he said it and cleared his throat. Detective Roberts, on the other hand, looked as calm as could be.

"You can't expect me to leave right now," I said, exasperated. "It's the dog show! I'm working all day. This is the busiest day of the year for me, and leaving now is out of the question." It was a ridiculous ask. On any other day it would be frustrating enough, but leaving the dog show, especially this early, was simply asking too much.

"This is a serious matter, Miss Potts," Detective Roberts said, taking a step forward. "We need you to come down to the station this very second."

"Well, unless you have a court order to drag me down there screaming, you're out of luck."

"Sibyl, please," Blake pleaded, still standing at the entrance of the grooming tent. I suspected that he wanted to be in this situation even less than I did. "Detective Roberts is right—this is serious. We need you to come with us. Please?" he added.

"Can you legally force me there?" I asked. If they could, I'd have no choice. Leaving the dog show immediately would be financially disastrous, but being dragged kicking and screaming by the police would probably be a tad worse.

Roberts cleared his throat as Blake shuffled uncomfortably. "I thought so," I said, annoyed at the whole thing. "So please let me get back to what I'm doing and I'll come around when I'm finished here."

"These charges are grave, Miss Potts," Detective Roberts said sternly. "Make sure you don't forget. I don't want to have to get a warrant of any kind, which is why I came here first."

"I get it, really," I said, sighing. "I'll be there as soon as I'm done."

The pair left me in peace, and I sat back down in my chair, breathing a sigh of relief. The rest of the day went smoothly enough, yet all I could think about was how I had to visit the police station. I was worried about what exactly was going to happen to me, as I imagined the police wouldn't show up at work unless they had a serious reason. Plus Detective Roberts had said something about having to get a warrant, which worried me even more.

Once the show was finally over, I drove straight to the police station, leaving my booth laid out as it was, meaning I'd have to come back and pack it up as soon as I was able. I had to trust that everything would work itself out and that, in my case, the police wouldn't arrest an innocent person.

When I arrived, a police officer I didn't recognise ushered me into an interrogation room. He sat me down and, politely enough, fetched me a cup of coffee. It didn't exactly taste great, being some sort of bitter brown water, but it was just barely better than nothing. I sat in the interrogation room for several minutes before Detective Roberts and Detective Henderson arrived and sat opposite me. Henderson shot me a weak smile, while Roberts maintained his best poker face.

"Can you tell me what this is about?" I asked, desperate to get this over with. My heart was pounding in my chest, and I wanted nothing more than to be at home. Of course, I knew this had to be something to do with Roland's death, but I didn't know any more than that.

"We know you were having an affair with Roland Cavendish," Detective Roberts said, leaning forward in his chair.

I was shocked. I looked at Henderson, though he was awkwardly staring at his feet instead of looking at me. "Why on earth do you think that?" I snapped. Roberts shot me an angry glare, but I couldn't care less. They had no idea what was going on.

"We have our sources," Roberts said, clearly not intending to clarify further.

"Well, your sources are ridiculous," I said. "I don't need to sit here and take this. I know you don't have evidence, because none of this is true. Besides, I have an alibi!"

"Yes, you said you were with Mr Buttons," Detective Roberts said, leaning forward. "Miss Potts, for all we know, Mr Buttons is covering for you."

"Why would he do that?" I asked. "This is all insane. Are you going to arrest me for something that you can't prove I did?"

"No, we're not going to arrest you—yet," Roberts said in a monotone. "We just need to ask you some questions."

"You've already asked me questions," I said, standing up. "I don't have the time or energy for this, especially when the accusation is so ridiculous. I'm all for doing whatever I can to catch whoever's responsible, but we're just wasting time here." I was embarrassed and frustrated that the detective accused me of having an affair with Roland.

"Sit down, Miss Potts. We'll detain you if we have to," Roberts said calmly.

I sat back down and crossed my arms, feeling myself getting angrier.

"I've got nothing more to tell you," I said with a shrug. "I was walking with Mr Buttons, and when I returned home, Roland was there, and he was dead. I don't know why he went into my home. To be honest, I'd assumed that figuring out that sort of thing was *your* job," I said with a glare of my own.

"Did you give him the ice cream sundae?" Roberts asked.

I shook my head. "No! As I've already told you, I invited his wife, Sally, over for one later in the day. I hadn't even prepared it."

Henderson looked up from making notes. "But you had purchased the ingredients?"

I nodded. "Sort of. I already had all the ingredients in the house."

The questioning continued for another couple of hours, though we were really just going over ground I'd already covered. I felt like Roberts was just doing this to spite me, since none of us really discovered anything new, except that police station coffee loses its flavour on about the seventh cup.

Eventually I was released, though Roberts was sure to let me know that they were keeping an eye on me and that I wasn't to leave town. They told me that I had to give them notification if I wanted to leave town, and that struck me as ridiculous.

Still, I decided that I should do as I was told, since I didn't want to give them any more reason to suspect me.

I drove back to my booth at the dog show and packed it away, wishing my day had gone better. I had been worried that somebody might have stolen something, but everything seemed to be in place when I returned, much to my relief.

I had almost finished packing when my phone rang. "Hello?" I said, resting the phone between my head and shoulder as I packed.

"Sibyl, it's Cressida," she explained, the concept of Caller ID apparently still foreign to her. "I just thought you'd like to know what Lord Farringdon said. It seems important."

I sighed. Lord Farringdon had been eerily accurate in the past, considering he was a cat, but it still bothered me that Cressida turned to him for information. "What is it?" I asked, figuring that it was better to ask than to ignore Cressida completely.

"He said that the killer is closer than we realised."

"Well, that's cryptic and unsettling," I said, sighing again. "Couldn't he just tell us who the killer is?"

"Oh, dear, no," Cressida said with a laugh, as if I'd asked the stupidest question possible.

"I'll have to talk to you later, Cressida," I said as I nearly dropped the stack of brushes I was balancing. "I'm cleaning up my booth. Thanks for the warning. I'll talk to you later." I freed a hand to end the call. I appreciated that she was trying to help, but her warning hadn't settled my nerves in any way.

I eventually managed to finish cleaning away my booth, much to my relief. Packing up was always the worst part of these kinds of jobs. I decided that I'd head to a café on my way home for a proper coffee to wash away the awful taste of whatever had passed for coffee back at the police station.

I stopped in at the first café I saw on the edge of town, ordering the strongest non-alcoholic drink they had, and sitting by the window. I took a moment to gather my thoughts. I did understand why the police had suspected me in the first place—after all, Roland had died in my own home. Yet had somebody tipped them off? If so, that person was likely the real murderer, or at least somebody who wanted the real murderer protected.

I was so lost in thought that I nearly missed it.

A man had come into the café and ordered take out, a fact of no interest until he walked out and got into a car with Sally. She laughed as the man said something to her, and I noticed he'd bought two coffees. Whoever he was, he was certainly good friends with Sally, who now seemed suddenly less concerned about the death of her husband. Still, the man hadn't paid any attention to me at all, so I doubted he knew who I was. But had Sally tipped off the police to try to frame me? It added up, but maybe I was over analysing. I took a long sip of my coffee and leant back in my chair. I needed a nap.

CHAPTER 6

"Oh, the poor roses," Mr Buttons lamented, picking off some leaves with black spots and throwing them onto the dirt.

"It *is* winter," I reminded him, gesturing to the landscape before us. The sky was overcast and with a grey tinge, not at all the brilliant deep blue of the familiar Australian sky. Some of the roses had managed to continue this late into winter, and the Sasanqua camellias were in full bloom. I pointed this out to Mr Buttons, but he did not seem consoled by the fact.

"Look at those dead trees!" he said, gesturing to a row of bare Alder trees on the horizon.

I shook my head. "You're from England," I

said. "You should be used to deciduous trees—you know they're not dead."

Mr Buttons rubbed his forehead in a gesture of sadness. "I expected to see these sights in England, but in Australia, I would expect that everything should be green and thriving all year-round."

I sighed. "You know as well as I do that that's the case on the coast, but here inland in the mountains, it gets as cold as it does in England in winter. I know the deciduous trees aren't native Australian trees, but..."

I broke off, not knowing where I was going with this train of thought. And I had to admit he was right. The landscape was bleak, depressing even. There was no pungent scent, no delicious aroma of perfumed flowers as there was in summer. The deciduous trees had lost the last of their pretty golden and red leaves, and now had bare limbs reaching out like hopeless spectres to the equally bleak sky. The camellias were the only flowering plants in the garden. Even the lavenders looked sad and were not flowering. The weeds, however, were entirely different matter. For some reason, they were flourishing.

My train of thought was broken by an angry

Dorothy bustling down the path. "What are you two doing here?" she demanded.

I held my breath, wondering how Mr Buttons would take her rude outburst. I didn't have to wait long. "Kindly desist from your unacceptable tone, madam," he said haughtily. "I do happen to live here, unless that fact has escaped your notice."

"Get back inside, the two of you!" Dorothy said.

Mr Buttons' face turned bright red, and his cheeks puffed up. He looked like a cartoon character who was about to explode. "How dare you address me in that unseemly manner? I shall do no such thing, of that I assure you," he said stonily.

I cast a hopeful look at the front door to see if Cressida would emerge. Cressida seemed to be the only one who could make Dorothy behave. I expect that was as she was her employer. Unfortunately, there was no sign of Cressida, but I turned as I heard the sound of the postman's motorbike.

Dorothy tried to push past Mr Buttons, but he stood his ground. "Get your hands off me!" she yelled at him.

Mr Buttons crossed his arms over his chest. "I

can assure you, madam, I have neither desire nor inclination to touch you."

I left them arguing and went to collect the mail. There was only one item, a large brown envelope addressed to Roland Cavendish. That would not have been surprising in itself, but what was surprising, was that the letters were glued on, just like the pages I had seen in movies where someone cuts out letters and glues them onto a ransom note.

I turned around to tell Mr Buttons about the strange envelope, when Dorothy lunged for it. I managed to pull it away just in time, and then Mr Buttons shouldered her out of the way.

"Quick, give me that letter," she insisted.

"No," I said firmly. "It's not addressed to you."

"It is addressed to a boarder, and *I* am the only staff member of the boarding house present." She said it quite viciously, and her eyes narrowed to slits.

Mr Buttons took the letter from me. "This letter is going straight to the police, madam," he said, "and you are raising my suspicions as to why you were so keen to get it. Maybe you have something to hide?"

Dorothy appeared to be summing up the situation for a moment, but then turned and stormed back up the path to the boarding house, muttering words that I had only ever heard my cockatoo utter previously.

Mr Buttons waited until Dorothy was safely inside before speaking. "Can you believe this, Sibyl? This looks like a blackmail letter. Who else would paste letters on like this? It was obviously sent before Roland died, and that's why Dorothy was so keen to get it before anyone else saw it."

I rolled my eyes. Mr Buttons had been sure that Dorothy was the murderer in every instance of murder at the boarding house—and, sad to say, there had been several. He was always completely and utterly convinced that Dorothy was the murderer. It seemed that this murder was no exception. "It must have been posted after he died, by someone who didn't know he was already dead," I pointed out.

Mr Buttons disagreed. "No, because it has a Little Tatterford postmark." He delicately jabbed his finger at the top right hand corner of the envelope.

I was puzzled. "What does that have to do with anything?"

"Obviously, everyone in town knows that Roland Cavendish had been murdered, so they are hardly likely to mail him a blackmail note after he's dead." Mr Buttons raised his eyebrows at me.

"But we don't know what's in the letter," I pointed out. "Maybe it was a student prank, or something."

Mr Buttons' face fell. "You're right. Of course, we need to read it! Let's go inside and open it."

"But we can't," I protested. "It's most likely evidence in a murder investigation."

Mr Buttons was unperturbed. "We'll use gloves when we steam it open," he pronounced triumphantly. "Let's go to your cottage, Sibyl, because we don't want Dorothy interfering, especially given the fact that she's the murderer."

I threw out my arms in exasperation, and followed Mr Buttons down to my cottage. What else could I do? I'd never convince him of the fact that Dorothy wasn't the murderer. He did not seem the least put out by the fact he had been proven wrong in every case previously. He just disliked the woman, and there was no getting around it.

I opened the door to my cottage, and hurried over to stoke the fire, with Mr Buttons hard on my heels. "If you want to know about mistakes, ask your parents!" came a voice behind us.

Mr Buttons jumped so hard that the envelope nearly fell into the fire. "Since when has Max spoken in such long sentences?" he asked me.

"He seems to be getting more fond of lengthy insults," I said with a sigh. "I suppose it's better than his usual string of profanities." Right on cue, Max uttered a string of said profanities.

I put the bird outside, trying not to listen to his foul language, no pun intended. Mr Buttons, resplendent in bright yellow gloves, had left the fire and was already boiling the electric kettle.

I hurried over to him. "Are you sure this is a good idea? You're tampering with evidence in a homicide investigation. Besides, it's freezing away from the fire."

By way of answer, Mr Buttons held the envelope over the steam from the electric kettle. "Have you checked the flue to make sure it's shut? That fire should warm your whole cottage."

"Yes, the flue's fine, but I think Cressida has changed her wood supplier. This wood doesn't warm the cottage as well as usual. You probably can't tell up at the boarding house because there are so many fires in it. I think it's stringy bark, whereas it used to be red gum. And it's green at that."

Mr Buttons didn't look up. Either he was bored by talk of firewood or he was too engrossed by tampering with evidence.

"You do realise I'm an accessory to this, don't you?"

I might as well have been speaking to a brick wall. Mr Buttons didn't respond, remaining intently focused on holding the envelope over the steam. After what seemed an age, he removed the envelope from the steam and carried it over to the counter. I hurried to place paper towels under the envelope. Mr Buttons carefully removed the contents, and laid them on a paper towel. I gasped.

There, written in individually pasted letters, were the words:

I know what you did. Go public with it at once, or die!

"It's a death threat!" I said, somewhat unnecessarily.

Mr Buttons picked up the envelope and peered at it. "The person who did this is not very tidy. See how these letters are scattered at angles?

And some letters are red, while some are black. The whole effect is that of untidiness."

"Like Dorothy would do?" I asked for a joke, and then instantly regretted it.

"Of course!" Mr Buttons exclaimed. "This is surely Dorothy's handiwork. She's a terribly messy woman." That was the worst insult Mr Buttons could muster. Before I could think of something to say, he pressed on. "The post mark is from a week ago."

"So it *was* posted before Roland died."

Mr Buttons nodded. "Yes, that seems to be the case."

"Just as well we didn't put our fingerprints on it," I said, "because we need to take this to the police."

"Yes, with great haste," Mr Buttons said. He gently put the letter back in the envelope, and then pushed it down hard so that it would stick. "Did you see how keen Dorothy was to get this envelope?" he asked me. "That just proves that she's the murderer."

"It doesn't prove anything," I said. "You *always* think that Dorothy's the murderer."

Mr Buttons looked somewhat embarrassed. "I know I was wrong before, but I'm absolutely convinced that she's the murderer this time." His tone was stubborn.

I shrugged. There was no use arguing with him. Nothing I could say would convince him that Dorothy was not the culprit. "Why don't we go to the Little Tatterford Post Office? They might remember who posted this."

Mr Buttons shook his head. "Whoever posted this wasn't likely to go into the Post Office and let people see the pasted-on letters. They would have posted it outside when no one was around."

I slapped myself on my forehead. "Of course! How silly of me."

"But we should still go to the Little Tatterford Post Office," Mr Buttons said. "They can at least tell us why a letter posted in the same town took a week to reach the boarding house. Maybe someone does know something, after all, something that will implicate Dorothy as the murderer."

I rolled my eyes. Just then, I heard something outside. "Is that a car?"

CHAPTER 7

Mr Buttons grabbed the envelope and put it behind his back. "No, I think it's thunder."

A knock on the front door proved him wrong. "Quick, hide the envelope!" I hissed. I hurried to the front door and flung it open.

It was Blake, but I hardly had a chance to see him before he pulled me to him and kissed me thoroughly. I clung to his warmth, and it took me a few moments to realise that Mr Buttons was still inside, not that I cared too much at that time.

"Get a room, you two!" Max squawked, and then he uttered a string of profanities that made Blake blush.

I spun around. "Mr Buttons, did you let Max

inside?" As soon as I said the words, I realised that he did that as a diversion to the envelope, although why simply hiding the envelope wouldn't have worked was beyond me.

Mr Buttons appeared and gave me an almost imperceptible nod. "I'll put Max outside."

When he returned, I asked him, "All taken care of?"

I felt bad deceiving Blake like that, but I had no choice. I could hardly admit that I had been tampering with evidence in a homicide investigation.

"We were just intending to call you," Mr Buttons said to Blake. He leant over the fire, and rubbed his hands together.

"You were? What about?" Blake likewise held his hands over the fire, and then turned to me. "Sibyl, is something wrong with your fire? It's not as warm as usual in here."

"It's the firewood," I said sadly. "Cressida's changed her firewood supplier." I wasn't taking any notice of Mr Buttons, the taste of Blake's kiss still lingering on my lips, when Mr Buttons thrust the envelope at Blake.

Blake jumped in surprise. "What's this?"

I hurried to explain. "The postman just brought this."

"We were just about to call you and tell you about it when you arrived here," Mr Buttons said. "Dorothy tried to stop the postman giving it to us. Why, she almost wrestled us to the ground to get the envelope from us. I find that very suspicious. I think you'll discover that Dorothy is the murderer."

Blake shot me a significant look. Clearly, he was just as tired of all the accusations against Dorothy as I was. I mean, the woman was highly unpleasant, but there was no need to think she was the perpetrator of every crime that had happened in Little Tatterford since her arrival.

Blake turned the envelope over. "Why did you bring this here instead of calling me at the boarding house?" he asked in a suspicious tone.

I desperately tried to think up something that sounded reasonable, but Mr Buttons beat me to it. "Because that mad woman, Dorothy, was doing her best to get the envelope from us, so I suggested to Sibyl that we go down to her cottage. Since Dorothy is the murderer, I didn't want the evidence to be near her. We were about to call you when we heard the knock. We only just arrived here and Sibyl got the fire going. Blake, the letter was postmarked over a week ago, but it was sent from Little Tatterford."

Blake raised his eyebrows. "It took over a week to get here and it was posted in the same town?"

Mr Buttons and I both nodded. Blake stared at me for a moment, and it was all I could do to hold his gaze and plaster what I hoped was an innocent look on my face. I was worried he'd come straight out and ask me if we had read the letter, but luckily he didn't. "So tell me exactly what happened, from the beginning."

"Sibyl and I were looking at the roses in the front garden of the boarding house, when the postman came. Dorothy took off like an Olympic sprinter and tried to snatch the envelope from Sibyl. When she couldn't get her grubby mitts on it, she demanded that we hand it over to her."

"Yes, that's right," I said. "I have to admit, Dorothy seemed keen to get the envelope."

Mr Buttons opened his mouth to speak, but Blake wisely got in first. "I'll take this down to the station and hand it over to the detectives," he said.

"Hopefully whatever's in it will help with the murder investigation," Mr Buttons said.

The look Blake shot us made me think that he

knew that we'd already steamed open the envelope. Still, he didn't give voice to his obvious suspicions, but merely left in a hurry, promising to be in touch soon.

"Why did you give it to him?" I asked Mr Buttons.

"Do you mind that I did?"

I shook my head. "No, we were going to give it to him, of course, but I wanted to show it to the post office lady first."

Mr Buttons pulled his iPhone from his pocket and smugly showed me photos of the letter.

"Well done, Mr Buttons," I said. "For a minute you had me worried. I wondered why you'd given the letter to Blake."

"I'm not as silly as I look," Mr Buttons said seriously.

I had no idea how to respond, so simply nodded. "Will we go to the post office now?"

Mr Buttons peered through the window and shuddered. "Might as well. I don't suppose there's any point waiting until it warms up."

I agreed. "We'd be here for months if we did that."

Fifteen minutes later, Mr Buttons and I were standing outside the Little Tatterford Post Office, deciding what to do. Well, we had already decided, but had changed our minds several times. Finally, I agreed to let Mr Buttons do the talking.

There were no other customers inside the small post office when we walked in. Carol, the post office manager, was at the counter. Mr Buttons took out his phone and showed her the photo of the envelope. "Carol, did you see anyone post this?"

She took his phone from him and turned it over, staring at the screen. "No, I don't remember anyone posting this. I sure would have remembered it, though."

"It was postmarked over a week ago, but it only arrived this morning," Mr Buttons told her. "Why would a letter posted in Little Tatterford take a week to arrive in Little Tatterford?"

"That's because Little Tatterford isn't a real post office," Carol said.

Mr Buttons and I exchanged glances. "What do you mean?" I asked her. It looked like a proper post office to me, and I had been sending letters from here ever since I had arrived in town. I had no idea what she meant. "Pharmidale is a real post office," she continued.

"I'm not sure I understand what you're saying," Mr Buttons said.

Carol shrugged. "It's like this. Little Tatterford is too small to have a proper post office like the one in Pharmidale, so everything posted here has to go to Pharmidale."

I was beginning to catch on. "So do you mean when something gets posted here, as it isn't considered to be a real post office, it has to go to a real post office first."

"Yes, that's right," Carol said. "That's the way post offices work in country New South Wales. If the letter is posted in Little Tatterford and addressed to somewhere else in Little Tatterford, the letter goes to Pharmidale, and then it goes to Sydney, and then it goes back to Pharmidale, and then back to Little Tatterford. That's the way Australia Post works."

"Why, that's quite insane!" I said.

Carol was quick to agree with me. "Yes it is, but that's Australia Post for you."

Mr Buttons leant over the counter to pick a piece of lint from Carol's coat. "So if a letter is posted in Little Tatterford to someone else to Little Tatterford, it could easily take a week to get there?"

Carol nodded. "Yes, that's right. A letter from England will get here faster."

My head spun with the craziness of it all.

Carol was still speaking. "And Australia Post has recently streamlined the service here." She made air quotes as she said the word 'streamlined.' "Now they only deliver mail every second day."

"You're kidding!" I said.

Carol shook her head. "I'm afraid not. Sad but true."

Before I could think of a suitable response, the two detectives burst through the door. I saw that Detective Roberts was clutching the envelope. "Mr Buttons!" I hissed urgently.

Mr Buttons put his phone in his pocket. "Five stamps, please. And don't mention what we just asked you, if you would be so kind," he added in a tone so low that I wasn't sure if Carol had heard him.

Mr Buttons handed over the cash for his stamps, at the same time bitterly complaining over the recently risen cost of stamps, and then both of us walked away to pretend to look at the merchandise. The detectives eyed us suspiciously, but continued on to the counter. Mr Buttons and I pretended not to be interested as the detectives questioned Carol about the envelope. She told them what she had told us, that the envelope was no doubt posted outside. She said she would ask the other two staff members if anyone had posted it over the counter, but the detectives agreed that they thought it unlikely.

Just as Mr Buttons and I had finished exclaiming over the tough bags and post packs, not to mention the very overdue Mother's Day cards that were still on display, I took Mr Buttons by the arm and indicated that we should leave.

Once outside the post office, we made a dash for my van. The sleet was coming down heavily now, little pieces of ice that stung as they pelted us viciously. It was a strange sort of cold here in this region of Australia, cold that permeated the bones, a cold that started inside, and that no amount of clothing would help.

I started the car and turned the heater to maximum, and waited for my teeth to stop chattering.

"That was a waste of time," Mr Buttons said sadly. "Dorothy wasn't silly enough to post it in person."

"Come on, Mr Buttons," I said. "We don't

know that it *was* Dorothy. Besides, Roland had only just arrived at the boarding house. The murderer must have expected him to arrive earlier, given the letter."

"Didn't you know?" Mr Buttons asked. "Roland and Sally were supposed to arrive last month. They were delayed, and Dorothy knew that they were coming."

"How did she know?" I asked in disbelief.

"The bookings are in the book at the front desk," he said smugly.

I shrugged. "It could just as easily have been his wife, trying to throw suspicion on someone else. You know, we really do have to consider the possibility that it was someone else. You always think the murderer is Dorothy, and it never has been."

Mr Buttons looked at me and frowned. "I know it's Dorothy," he said, "but we do have a more pressing problem."

"What's that?" I asked in alarm.

Mr Buttons frowned so hard that I expected his eyebrows to shoot from his forehead. "Cressida's art showing in Little Tatterford tonight."

CHAPTER 8

"Oh, boy," I said, trying my best to smile. "It sure is something."

Cressida smiled warmly. "Thanks, Sibyl! A lot of people have liked it so much that their jaws literally dropped," she said excitedly.

I wasn't at all surprised, as it had taken an enormous amount of willpower to stop myself from running away and screaming. I thought I'd eventually get used to Cressida's art, but it seemed as though she managed to make each piece more terrifying than the last.

This particular painting was, apparently, a detailed illustration of the sacking of Troy. Cressida had told me as much before I'd seen it, so naturally I'd assumed the painting would focus on a giant wooden horse. Instead, she had decided to focus on how the Trojans were massacred, in excruciating detail. To her credit, the detail was astounding, but it made the piece awfully hard to look at for any extended period of time.

"There's no wooden horse," I pointed out when she stopped to draw breath.

Cressida frowned. "Of course not, Sibyl. Only Virgil's *Aeneid* mentioned the wooden horse. You'll find no mention of any wooden horse in Homer's *Iliad,* and Homer's account of the Trojan War is centuries earlier than Virgil's. I've based this painting on the *Iliad*, and I quote, 'Telemon's son leaped forward and struck him on his bronze helmet. The plumed headpiece shattered at the point of the weapon, struck at once by the spear and by Ajax's strong hand so that his blood-covered brain came oozing out through the crest…'"

"Okay!" I said a little too loudly as I clutched at my stomach. I finished my almost-full glass of wine as quickly as I could, hoping it would take the edge off being surrounded by visions and sounds of existential dread. It did. I figured more couldn't hurt. As I selected another glass of wine, Cressida excitedly told me about all the compliments she had received.

"Some people are telling me that they've never seen work quite like this before," she explained.

I believed it. "I'm glad you're doing so well, Cressida. Where's Mortimer?" I asked, looking around for Cressida's art dealer. He had been responsible for setting up this exhibition, though of course Cressida had also put in a considerable amount of time and effort making sure it ran smoothly. To their credit, they had done an admirable job, and while the art itself made the entire event feel like some kind of horror show, the venue was large, open, clean, and fancy. There were various kinds of wines and champagnes served along with light snacks, including more varieties of cheese than I realised even existed.

"Oh, he's around somewhere," Cressida said absent-mindedly. "He'd be very busy talking to people, I suppose. I should be as well, but I'm just too excited!"

I could see that she was telling the truth by the quiver in her voice and by the way her hands shook as she spoke. I was glad that she was having such a good time with the whole event. "Have you sold anything yet?" I asked her. I hoped she had, or the question might be a bit hurtful. I wouldn't have asked at all, except after meeting Mortimer, I discovered that people were entirely happy to buy Cressida's art, despite the horror of it all. I had just assumed that they were using her art to scare away unwanted guests.

Cressida beamed. "Oh, yes, actually. Quite a few, though, to be honest, it's a bit of a worry, as we hadn't planned to sell so many. Replacing them might be a bit of an issue for the gallery, so I have a lot of work ahead of me," she said, clearly not at all worried despite having said she was just a second ago.

"That's great news, Cressida," I said between mouthfuls of some strange food I hoped was a kind of cheese. "I'm really happy for you."

Cressida gave me an unexpected hug that was far too tight, but thankfully released me before I passed out from lack of oxygen. "Thanks, Sibyl! Anyway, I had better go find Mortimer and talk to snooty art people." She seized a new glass of wine and hurried off into the crowd.

I looked up at a nearby artwork and nearly lost my recently devoured cheese. The painting was uncomfortably gory, and displayed several heads on pikes in front of a terrifying Gothic castle. It was titled, 'Vlad the Impaler.' I overheard a woman behind me remark that this piece was "a little toned down compared to the others," and that it "lacked the forcefulness that carried her other works to such great heights." If I were to critique it, my thoughts would be more along the lines of, "Why would any sane person want to look at this?"

To be fair to Cressida, she was in fact skilled as a painter. Actually, that was mostly my problem, as the mortifying scenes she depicted were much too lifelike and detailed, which is why I was so uncomfortable. I considered suggesting that she try something more abstract for her next series. A lot more abstract.

Looking around the room, I wasn't able to spot anybody I recognised. I was still astounded at the sheer number of people who had decided to attend the exhibition. I wasn't even aware that the Pharmidale district had such a large population of those who enjoyed art, much less those who enjoyed this kind of art. Still, I was happy for Cressida, especially since it all seemed to be going so well.

Despite all that, I couldn't help but be a little disappointed that Blake hadn't been able to make it tonight. He was busy working. I sighed and scanned the room again. I hadn't just come to the exhibition to support Cressida, or to support the wine, for that matter. A huge number of people from around town were at the event, and I was hoping to gather as much information as I possibly could about Sally and that man. They say that it's always the spouse, so I thought that it was as good a place as any to begin investigating.

Here I was again, investigating a murder. Still, if the police were going to suspect me, then I couldn't risk leaving it alone, so long as I didn't do anything to incriminate myself in the process. *The police really should start paying me at this point*, I thought grimly, sipping another tall glass of expensive wine.

Before I could drink too much more, I spotted Sally Cavendish talking to a stranger across the room. I gulped and thought about what to say. Could I even talk to her? What if she'd heard that I was a suspect in Roland's murder? After the way

Roland had been treating her, would she even care? I sighed, and walked over to her. I waited just out of sight until she broke off her conversation with the person to whom she was speaking, and took my chance to get some information out of her. Carefully.

"Hi, Sally," I said, mustering the most earnest smile I could manage.

"Oh, hello," she said, smiling back. She seemed calm enough, I thought. Maybe even too calm, considering what had happened to Roland.

"Are you enjoying the exhibition?" I asked, suddenly unsure of how I was going to swing the conversation back to Roland. Talking about somebody's dead husband was harder than I'd realised, which seemed silly in hindsight.

"Yes, though the artwork is a bit... different," Sally replied, glancing nervously at a painting of the Normandy beach landings. "Cressida is a very gifted artist, though," she continued politely.

"It's okay," I laughed. "The art scares everybody. Well, I thought it did, but here we are." I motioned to the crowd of reverent art critics. I realised then that I wasn't going to be able to talk about Roland to her. If she were somehow involved, she'd be very much on guard, and if she weren't involved, I was likely to upset her and cause a scene rather than gather any meaningful information. I decided to try a different, more honest route.

"I was getting an afternoon coffee at a café on the edge of Pharmidale yesterday and saw a man I didn't recognise get into a car with you." Nerves caused me to speak quickly, and I wondered if Sally had managed to catch everything I'd said. "I just wanted to make sure you were okay after everything that's happened with Roland," I continued lamely, hoping she didn't think I was accusing her of anything. Not yet, anyway.

"Oh," she stammered, looking down at her feet. "I..."

"Thanks for coming, everybody," Cressida said through a microphone as the lights dimmed. Sally and I turned to see Cressida standing on a small stage, addressing the crowd. "I'm not one for public speaking, so I'll try to keep it brief." Cressida cleared her throat. I looked over to see that Sally had gone. A quick scan through the crowd didn't reveal her whereabouts. Had she left to avoid answering my question?

"I'm excited to be able to display my artworks in public like this," Cressida continued, motioning vaguely to the entire room, where each wall was covered in something she had painted. "But I'm more excited to have people talk to me about them, so please don't be afraid to approach me and ask questions about the pieces at any point tonight."

I considered that people would have many questions, and maybe I myself could even ask some, but most of the questions I had stored away would probably offend her. The paintings still scared and baffled me, so the less I had to talk about them, the better.

"Before I step off the stage, I'm often asked why I paint the subjects that I do," Cressida said. I stopped thinking and looked at her intently, hoping for an answer, though I was a little worried about what her explanation might be. "It's very simple, of course. Lord Farringdon, my cat, tells me what to paint," she said, beaming. The crowd laughed, which confused Cressida, judging by the look on her face. She stepped off the stage and was immediately swamped by people wanting to ask her questions. I considered rescuing her from the adoring legion, but decided she was probably enjoying the attention.

"Oh, Sibyl!"

I spun around to see Prudence Paget standing behind me, a wide smile on her face. She had a nearly-finished glass of wine, and had clearly been here for a while.

"Oh, hello, Prudence," I said, returning the smile. "Enjoying the exhibition?"

"Yes, very much. I had no idea that Cressida did so much painting," Prudence said, momentarily looking at a nearby artwork before averting her gaze and looking ill, if only for a brief second.

I sighed, deciding that the direct approach was all that was available to me. "Do you know if Sally has a boyfriend?" I asked.

Prudence's eyebrows shot up in surprise. "Oh, well, no," she said, taken aback by my question. "I mean, Roland just died, so..."

"It's just, I saw her in a car with a man, and they seemed awfully friendly," I continued. "I don't mean to be suggesting anything unsavoury. I'm just worried about her. Plus I don't know her so well, so maybe she has a relative or friend in town, or something." I shrugged.

"I'm afraid I don't know, Sibyl," Prudence said flatly. "Are you sure it was her?"

I shrugged. I supposed I wasn't sure, really, though the resemblance was uncanny. I downed the last of my wine and decided that the night had been a bust, at least for information gathering. I heard a laugh erupt from the crowd and consoled myself with the fact that at least Cressida's night had gone well.

CHAPTER 9

"Come in, come in!" Cressida smiled broadly as the boarding house filled with guests. She had decided to invite several people from the exhibition back to the boarding house to continue the event and to have a look at the art work that she had not yet displayed. The boarding house was packed to capacity, and it struck me as odd that so many people were willing to come back to the boarding house for Cressida's art.

Not that I didn't appreciate that her art was skilful, and I certainly knew that she had a paying audience. I had just assumed that a lot of the people at the gallery were there for an initial look, so it took me by surprise when they happily followed Cressida back home.

Shortly after her speech, she had gotten back on stage and announced that the boarding house was open for those who wanted to 'keep the party going,' as she put it. She had nearly fallen off the stage afterward, so I assumed some expensive gallery wine also had a say in the idea, but either way, she'd won over the crowd. Almost everybody had agreed to come back, and we'd walked the entire way in one massive group. A select few had decided to drive, though the majority weren't quite sober enough.

I had decided to walk alongside Mr Buttons, whom I hadn't seen at all during the gallery showing itself, but had spotted while I was following Cressida outside—or, more accurately, followed the mob that had surrounded her. It was a bit surreal to see Cressida being treated as some kind of celebrity all of a sudden, but I was happy for her. I was less happy for the boarding house, which didn't seem to be built for this kind of enormous crowd. The dining room was packed to capacity, and I very much doubted that most of the people here would be able to so much as glimpse any of Cressida's work.

Still, the atmosphere was pleasant and excited, yet I suspected it would start to falter fairly quickly since the boarding house didn't provide any kind of alcohol.

"Well, I'm glad she's doing so well," Mr Buttons said, smiling broadly. "I'm not as happy about having such a large crowd in our humble abode, but it's for a good cause."

"I'd hardly call the boarding house a humble abode," I said with a laugh. Looking around, though, the huge crowd certainly made everything look a lot smaller. "I see your point, though," I admitted.

"Hello, Sibyl, Mr Buttons," Sally said from behind, causing me to jump.

"Oh, hello, Sally," Mr Buttons said with a warm smile. "Were you at the show, too?"

"I was," she said with a nod. "Cressida certainly is popular. Or rather, her art is, I suppose."

"Yes, she's doing really well," I agreed. "It's good to see her being happy and successful. There was a point where..."

"What is all this?" A shout sounded out from the kitchen, a shout so loud that the windows shook violently. It was Dorothy, her face redder than a human face had any business turning. She was shaking with rage and just about frothing at the mouth. "Who are you people?" she screamed, throwing a spoon at an unfortunate witness.

"Who's she?" Sally whispered to me. "I've seen her before. Is she the cook?"

"Yes, she's the boarding house cook," I replied, refraining from explaining that she was also quite possibly some kind of deep-sea monster given human form in an ungodly bargain. "You've probably seen her around the boarding house, especially during meal times."

Sally nodded.

"If you've seen *Free Willy*, you might have her mistaken for the whale," Mr Buttons said scathingly.

"Mr Buttons!" I scolded him. "You can't say things like that," I said as Sally managed to suppress a giggle.

There was more yelling from Dorothy's general direction, and it was clear that whoever was talking to her had come to an impasse. Dorothy pushed through the crowd and stormed out of the boarding house, leaving a large confused crowd in her wake.

"I should be going to bed, anyway," Sally said with a yawn. "I hope that lady's okay."

"She'll be fine." I smiled reassuringly. "This isn't the first time she's done this kind of thing. I think she might just be nervous around crowds, or just... well, just angry." I shrugged. "We're not really sure what the story is. Anyway, goodnight, Sally."

Sally nodded to us as she walked away in the direction of the stairs to her room.

"She did it," Mr Buttons said with a stern nod.

"What, Sally?" I asked, raising an eyebrow. "You think she murdered Roland?" I tried to lower my voice as I asked, though the bustling crowd made it hard to be quiet. Mr Buttons beckoned me to follow him out into the front yard where the noise was considerably less intrusive.

"No, no, Dorothy," he said in a harsh whisper. "She's the guilty one, Sibyl, mark my words."

"What makes you say that now?" I asked. "Have you uncovered some evidence?"

"Because it seems like something she'd do," he said calmly, as if it were the most logical explanation in the world.

I sighed loudly and pointedly. "That's hardly reason to suspect her, Mr Buttons."

"All the same, it's true," he said, literally turning his nose up at me.

I playfully punched him in the arm and laughed. "She's guilty of all sorts of things, I'm sure, but I think we should look elsewhere in this case. Speaking of which, the police told me that they don't have enough evidence of my alibi," I explained, not wanting to drag the mood down, but needing to get it off my chest.

"But that's absurd." Mr Buttons gave me his full attention again. "I was right there with you, Sibyl. You couldn't possibly be involved, and neither could I."

"I know," I said with a nod. "But the police have no proof of that. It's just our word they're relying on, after all."

Mr Buttons considered the situation for a moment and sighed. "I suppose that's true. Cressida really ought to have some security cameras installed by now," he said with a small laugh, though he looked more worried than anything else.

"I'm sure the police will clear this up. After all, you and I both know that we're innocent, because we weren't anywhere near Roland when he died. All the same, it's probably best if we don't do anything that looks suspicious," I said, hoping Mr Buttons would take my words to heart. It didn't seem right that we had to avoid suspicion when we were innocent, but I'd much rather do so than be arrested for a crime, especially one that I didn't commit.

The other guests slowly departed, leaving the boarding house feeling both emptier and larger than it ever had before. I was amazed at how polite and clean everybody had been. As far as I could tell, not a single piece of furniture was out of place.

Mr Buttons was fetching us all tea. Mortimer had stayed behind, and was busily chatting to Cressida at the dinner table.

"So, how did the exhibition go?" I asked. It seemed like it had been a resounding success, but then it occurred to me that I didn't really know what kind of reception they were expecting. Besides that, I wasn't actually sure how to start a conversation with Mortimer, a man about whom I knew so little.

"It was fantastic, Sibyl." Cressida beamed as she spoke.

"A much better reception than I'd expected," Mortimer admitted in his usual monotone voice. "I was expecting great things, of course, but it was still an exceptional turn out. And the sales." His eyebrows shot up as he said it, though the tone of his voice didn't change despite the elevation in volume. If I hadn't seen him excited in the past, I'd have wondered if he had some kind of condition where he had to speak as monotonously as possible.

CHAPTER 10

"Come on, Sandy." I tried to put a dog coat on the reluctant Labrador. She wanted to stay in her dog bed. It was so cold that I almost thought about crawling in there with her. I checked the time, and saw to my dismay that Mr Buttons was late for our morning walk. Perhaps he shared the same view of the dismal weather as Sandy.

I was throwing more wood on the fire when I heard Mr Buttons arrive. I opened the door to see him holding a delicate porcelain plate filled with cucumber sandwiches with, of course, the crusts removed, as well as a plate of pastries. "Are we having breakfast before we walk?" I asked him.

His face fell. "Sibyl, it's far too cold to walk."

He placed the plates on the coffee table, and then hurried over to warm himself at the fire. "I don't think we should walk today. The forecast is for heavy snow. That's why it was warmer last night. It always warms up a little in these parts before it snows or rains."

I shivered at the thought. "You're right. Shall we have coffee, cucumber sandwiches, and pastries instead?"

Mr Buttons turned around, beaming. "Yes, what a good idea. You make the tea and I'll dust."

I shook my head and went to do as I was told, while Mr Buttons eagerly dusted the floor around the fire.

I soon returned with two steaming mugs—tea for Mr Buttons and coffee for me—and placed them on the coffee table next to the cucumber sandwiches and pastries.

Mr Buttons abandoned his dusting to take a seat opposite me. "Let's investigate Dorothy's connection with the vic."

I was momentarily puzzled. "Who's Vic?"

Mr Buttons sighed deeply. "Not Vic, *the* vic. The victim, Roland. They must be connected in some way."

I never was a morning person, and this wasn't

making much sense to me. I took a large gulp of coffee in an attempt to get the caffeine into me as quickly as possible. "Why would Dorothy be connected with the vic?"

Mr Buttons sighed again. "Quite obviously, Sibyl," he said in a patronising tone, "there must be a connection between them, or why would she murder him?"

"She didn't murder him," I said, exasperated. "We're wasting time. We should be focusing on the real killer, or better still, leaving that to the detectives."

Mr Buttons pointed to his mouth to indicate that he was still eating. When he had finished, he said, "I insist upon investigating Dorothy for a connection with the vic."

I shrugged. I knew when I was beaten. After all, he had brought food. "Okay then, you win," I said over my shoulder as I went to fetch my laptop.

"I think the saying, my screen is frozen, has taken on a whole new meaning," I said as I brought out my laptop. I was glad I was wearing fingerless gloves because the metal was almost too cold to touch.

I put it on the coffee table and then pulled the

coffee table closer to the fire. "Is this warm enough in here for you, Mr Buttons?"

Mr Buttons shook his head. "You've got the fire going nicely, but I suspect the wood is green. This will probably be as good as it gets. Now, do you remember when we got Dorothy's résumé and checked her last employer?"

I nodded. How could I forget? Mr Buttons had been sure that Dorothy had been the murderer of Lisa Summers. However, Lisa actually had been murdered by her husband, Greg, so that he could get his hands on a multi-million dollar property deal. Mr Buttons had gone so far as to obtain CCTV footage in an attempt to prove that Dorothy was the murderer. He was wrong, of course. And then there was the murder of Sue, a boarder. Once again, Mr Buttons had been convinced that the murderer was Dorothy, but it had turned out to be James, the leader of a ghost-hunting investigative group. On that occasion, Mr Buttons had made me accompany him on a long drive to question Dorothy's last employer. He was upset when James, rather than Dorothy, was proven to be the murderer, and it was small comfort to him that Dorothy turned out to be James's aunt. He kept insisting that his tarot cards always provided portents of doom about Dorothy's character.

I looked up as Mr Buttons spoke again. "All we have to do is find a lot of information on Roland Cavendish, and see if that connects in any way with Dorothy."

"And with any of the other suspects," I said with a grimace.

Mr Buttons set down his tea cup loudly, clanging it in the saucer. "What other suspects do we have?"

"Roland's wife, Sally, and of course, Prudence Paget. I already told you that I saw Sally in Pharmidale with a man."

Mr Buttons waved my comments away. "We already know that Sally and Prudence have connections to Roland. That's obvious!"

"Yes, and that's my point," I said. Still, I knew nothing would get in the way of Mr Buttons' convictions that Dorothy was the murderer.

Mr Buttons stared at the computer for some minutes, while I warmed myself by the fire. Suddenly, he stood up. "Look at this! Dorothy was in Sydney for three years. Roland was in Sydney at the same time!"

"So were about five million other people," I

pointed out. "But remember, Dorothy's real name is Samantha something."

"Samantha Dorothy Hicks," Mr Buttons said angrily. "I know everyone thinks James killed Sue because she threatened to expose that he'd faked his ghost-hunting evidence, and so he'd lose out on that big television deal, but I think Dorothy was in it with him."

I sighed. "Dorothy was the one who tipped us off."

Mr Buttons nodded solemnly. "Yes, to cover her own…"

"$#%@" said Max, finishing Mr Buttons' sentence for him.

"How did you get in?" I asked him, and was at once met with a tirade of verbal abuse. I seized the bird and put him outside once more, then firmly latched the back door. When I returned, Mr Buttons was cross-checking Dorothy's original name against Roland's name.

"Anything?" I asked him.

He shook his head. "I've drawn a blank."

"What about checking the name of Dorothy's husband?"

"That woman had a husband?" Mr Buttons asked with exaggerated disbelief.

"Yes, don't you remember? On one of the occasions when you were so sure that Dorothy was the murderer, we came across a blog post where she said her husband had run off with another woman, and that's why she changed her name."

"The man obviously had good sense," Mr Buttons said. He was about to say more, when there was a knock on the door.

I opened the door to be met with a cold blast to my face. Tiny little pieces of sleet stung me. I wiped the sleet from my eyes to see Detective Roberts standing there, his hands on his hips.

"Come in," I said. I invited him in mainly because it was too cold to stand there with the door open. He walked past me, and so did Detective Henderson, who was standing right behind him.

They wasted no time coming to the point. "I need to question you now," Roberts said, and then he noticed Mr Buttons sitting by the fire. The two detectives exchanged glances.

"Good to find you here," Henderson said to Mr Buttons. "I was about to go to the boarding house to question you."

Mr Buttons just glared at him.

"Please accompany me now to the boarding house for questioning," Henderson continued.

"Why can't you question me here?" Mr Buttons said sulkily. "It's too cold to go outside."

Henderson crossed his arms over his chest. "We will drive. We need to question the two of you separately. You could come down to the station, if you prefer."

Mr Buttons' face turned red at the obvious threat. "All right then, I'll go with you, but please note that I am coming under protest."

He muttered some more words, and at first I thought Max had come back inside and was up to his usual language. My ears burned when I realised it was Mr Buttons. As soon as Detective Henderson and Mr Buttons were out the door, Detective Roberts walked once more to the fire and held his hands over it. "Your cottage isn't very warm, is it?"

"It's warmer than outside," I said, none too kindly.

Detective Roberts did not respond, but pulled out the chair that Mr Buttons had vacated and sat on it opposite me. "We have been informed that you were, in fact, having an affair with Roland Cavendish by someone who saw the two of you together. What do you have to say about that?"

I flushed with anger. "They're lying! That's not true. I've already told you that, and if someone has actually told you such a thing, then they're obviously the murderer, so I suggest you look at them." I was beyond furious. I couldn't believe that the cops had come to ask me a question on a tip off by someone who was probably the murderer. I mean, who else would have a reason to make up such an outrageous claim?

"And do you still maintain that you and Mr Buttons were walking and returned to your cottage to find the victim on the floor, along with an ice cream sundae?"

"Yes, that's exactly what happened."

"And you and Mr Buttons didn't cook up that story?"

I jumped to my feet. "I've told you the absolute truth, and Mr Buttons would have told you the very same absolute truth, too. I had invited Roland's wife, Sally, to my cottage for an ice cream sundae later in the day. When I got there, I found Roland dead."

Detective Roberts stood up and rubbed his hands over the fire once more. "And why would you offer anyone an ice cream sundae in this weather?"

"I don't know!" I snapped. "I happen to like chocolate, ice cream, and coffee, and I eat ice cream all through winter, and I drink coffee all through summer. Is that so strange?"

"Yes, it is rather strange," he remarked.

"What is strange?" I was no longer intimidated by the detective—rather, I was angry. I knew that he was only doing his job, but from my point of view, I was quite irritated. I took a deep breath and tried to calm down. "Are you telling me you don't drink coffee in summer?"

"I'm not here to answer questions," Robert said, although not unkindly. "It just seems awfully strange that you would invite Cavendish's wife for an ice cream sundae in the thick of winter, with snow and sleet outside."

"Well, surely Sally Cavendish told you I had invited her?"

The detective did not respond, but I could see that she had. Otherwise, I'm sure that he would've told me so.

"And you were seen purchasing antifreeze the day before the murder."

That threw me. "Uh, what, what?" I stammered.

"Antifreeze," Roberts said. "Coolant, glycol, propylene glycol. You were seen in Little Tatterford purchasing the substance."

"So?" I said. "Doesn't everybody? In this climate, the radiator cracks if you don't put antifreeze in it. That's common knowledge." It took a moment or two for the realisation to hit me. Roland was poisoned with antifreeze, or at least that's how it was beginning to look.

Roberts continued. "Can you tell me about your friends?"

I wasn't sure what he meant, but I thought I should answer as best I could. "Cressida and Mr Buttons are my two closest friends," I said.

"What about Sergeant Wessley?"

I could feel my cheeks burning hot, and I knew for a fact that a guilty look had passed across my face. "What do you mean?"

"Are you and Sergeant Wessley in a romantic relationship?" The question came out as an accusation, or so it seemed to me.

"Um, err..." I stammered. What should I say? What if Blake had already denied it? I supposed he had not, as he himself was a police officer.

"Well, we've had dinner together, so we're sort of dating."

I held my breath, thinking that Roberts would cross-examine me, but to my relief, he pressed on. "Now to the morning of the murder. You say you woke up, got your dog, and went out to meet Mr Buttons to take your dog for a walk?"

"Yes."

"And the body was not there then."

"Of course not!" I said angrily. "Do you really think I did it?"

"We have to ask questions of everyone," he said, "especially of those who found the body and alleged they were out walking when the murder happened."

"What motive would I possibly have?" I asked him.

He shook his head. "You've been watching too much American TV. We don't have to have a motive to charge someone with murder in Australia. Would you like to tell me what happened?"

I rubbed my temples. "I've already told you a thousand times."

"So what was it that pushed you over the edge, Ms Potts? What was it that made you kill? I think I know. You were having an affair with a married man, Roland Cavendish, but your eye strayed to the person of Sergeant Blake Wessley. You thought you needed to get rid of Roland before he could tell Sergeant Wessley about your frequent assignations."

Just then, there was another knock at the door. I assumed it was Detective Henderson, but when Roberts made no move to answer it, I did so. It was Blake. My stomach reeled. "Are you looking for Detective Roberts?" I said at once, thankfully that I had been so quick-witted. I held the door back so Blake could see him.

The two of them exchanged glances, and the looks were far from friendly. "I'm here on a personal matter," Blake said after a lengthy pause. "Are you finished here?" The latter comment was to Roberts.

"For now." Roberts excused himself and hurried out the door. I unkindly hoped he would freeze on his way to the boarding house.

CHAPTER 11

"You look lovely."

I blushed, smiled, and took my seat opposite Blake in the restaurant. Blake had said he would meet me there at seven because he had to work until the last minute and thought he might be late. As it turned out, he got there before I did. He hadn't stayed long after he had interrupted Detective Roberts questioning me, and had simply come to ask me to dinner that night.

I had taken special care with my appearance even though I had to wrap up and add layers of coats and scarves. I was pleased that Blake had reserved a table right next to the roaring log fire. It might not have been the most intimate part of the restaurant, but it sure was the warmest. As usual, my stomach fluttered wildly in Blake's presence and I forced myself to take deep breaths, albeit subtle ones.

I shivered as I sat down, and Blake at once offered me his coat. I declined, saying that I would soon warm up. In fact, soon after I had taken off my coat, the heat from the fire became as overbearing as it was welcome.

The normally overcrowded restaurant was rather bereft of patrons, and I wondered why. I supposed it was something to do with the weather, although I figured that the locals would be well used to it, more used to it than I was. Or perhaps there was something good on TV. Whatever the reason, I was grateful for the privacy.

Before I even had a chance to look at the menu, Blake reached across the table and took my hand. My heart beat out of my chest, and I hoped he couldn't feel me shaking.

"Sibyl, there's something I have to tell you."

All of a sudden I was terrified. A thousand different fears sparked like fireworks through my mind. Surely he wasn't going to break up with me? Surely not. I mean, he *was* holding my hand,

and we had only just started dating. A faint wave of nausea washed over me.

"Sibyl, you're the detectives' main suspect."

A mix of emotions coursed through me. I didn't know whether I should be pleased or upset. Sure, I was relieved that Blake wasn't breaking up with me, but I wasn't too thrilled that the police saw me as the main suspect. I had watched enough documentaries on the crime channel to know that innocent people were convicted of murder every day. Well, perhaps not every day, but it certainly wasn't an uncommon occurrence.

I nodded slowly. Blake continued. "And Detective Roberts tore strips off me for dating you."

"Why? That's hardly illegal."

Blake shrugged. "That's what I told him. I told him we started dating well before he considered you a prime suspect." He held up his hands, which unfortunately meant that he let go of mine. "Rest assured, I told him in no uncertain terms that there is no way you're a murderer."

"But he didn't believe you." I said it as a statement, not a question.

Blake hesitated, but then shook his head. "I'm afraid not. He thought I was too involved and so had lost perspective. But don't you worry, there's no way I'm going to let him charge you for something you didn't do, especially something as serious as murder."

Warmth flooded my bones, and it wasn't from the fire. I was relieved that Blake was looking out for me. At that moment, I felt safe and protected. Still, I couldn't shake the fact that the detectives really saw me as a suspect in the murder case. "Do you have any idea who did it?" I asked Blake.

"Not yet, but I'm looking into it. Of course, that's just between us. I'm not officially allowed to look into it."

I nodded. "Thanks, Blake." I was dismayed that my voice was shaking. I wanted to ask about the antifreeze, but I didn't want to put Blake in an uncomfortable position.

At that point, I looked up to see a waiter hovering over us. I chose a Thai red curry. I always preferred Thai green curry, but it wasn't on offer. Blake chose something with steak, fennel, orange, and beet. The animated waiter, with an accompanying wave of his arms, said something about it being a great combination of flavours and that it was aromatic. I wasn't really listening, because I had more pressing matters on my mind. I silently lectured myself to forget about the murder investigation and the fact that I was a suspect for the night, and instead enjoy Blake's company.

We ate the meal in silence, and I had the uneasy feeling that Blake wanted to say more to me. I was proven right. He set down his fork, and looked up at me once more. "Sibyl, I don't think we should have dinner again until the murder is solved."

"You mean we shouldn't see each other?" If I had thought before I had spoken, I probably would have said something far more subtle, but at least this way I would get a straight answer.

"That sounds bad when you put it like that," Blake said. "I just mean we shouldn't do anything to give the detectives a reason to…" He hesitated.

"A reason to do what?" I asked him.

Blake shrugged, and I jumped when the fire made a popping sound and a spark flew out. "I don't really know. Roberts told me that it's not appropriate for a member of the local police force to date a suspect."

"Sure, I don't want to make things difficult for you," I said, trying to keep the disappointment out of my voice.

Blake shook his head. "You misunderstand

me. It's not myself I'm worried about, I'm worried about you. I don't want to make things more difficult for you."

I nodded.

"The detectives are stumped in this matter," he continued, "and because you found the body, in their eyes you're the prime suspect. They don't have anything else to go on. My concern is that they'll think I'm covering for you. If we're seen to be dating, then they might be harder on you."

I nodded again. Blake's words made sense, but I was disappointed.

Blake reached forward to take my hands again. "It won't be long, Sibyl. I'm sure they'll find the murderer soon."

"Not if they keep concentrating on me," I said sadly.

Blake appeared to be about to say something, but then returned to his meal. My excitement about what had held the promise of a great night had now turned to distress. On the bright side, Blake hadn't broken up with me, but I couldn't shake the feeling that he had. I wondered if that was the real reason that he had wanted us to meet at the restaurant. Logically, he was right that we shouldn't see each other until the murder investigation was over, but logic wasn't cheering me up at that moment.

I excused myself and went to the bathroom. I was about to return when I received a text from Mr Buttons. *Tomorrow. Quoll woman. University of Pharmidale.*

I texted back to ask him what he meant. He responded at once. *Prudence giving lecture on quolls. We must go 2 c if she had grudge against vic. We will snoop. I'm investigating someone other than Dorothy. U should be pleased.*

I smiled. That would take my mind off things, and who knows, perhaps we would turn up something to implicate Prudence. The only drawback was having to sit through what I anticipated would be a boring lecture.

We continued to eat in silence until the waiter brought the dessert menus. I chose the first thing I saw, a fruit sorbet with chocolate ganache and meringue shard. The waiter was excited about my choice. He said it looked wonderful, was refreshing, and provided a superb finish to a meal. He said something about dehydrated grapefruit, but again, I wasn't paying attention.

The waiter was more excited about Blake's choice. "A chocolate tangelo explosion!" he exclaimed. "It's salty, sweet, sour, fresh, acidic, with the chocolate flavour front and centre, along with the gingerbread and the flavour of tangelo. The texture ticks a lot of boxes!" He beamed, and then hurried away.

"Don't worry," Blake said. "I'm looking into the murder. I won't let them arrest you."

"Thanks." I forced a smile. "Mr Buttons thinks it's Dorothy."

Blake laughed. "Mr Buttons always thinks it's Dorothy."

I shrugged. "He could be right this time."

Blake leant across the table. "Why do you say that?"

I laughed in spite of myself. "Actually, only because it's not me. At this point, I want the detectives to find the murderer—anyone that's not me will suit me just fine. But seriously, Blake, do you have any suspects at all?"

He hesitated, and I wondered at first if he was keeping something from me. "Only Sally Cavendish and Prudence Paget. The detectives really need to focus on them."

I nodded. "That's for sure. I suppose you know that the detectives had a tip off that I was having an affair with Roland? Can you find out who told them that? Whoever it was would have to be the murderer."

Blake shook his head. "They probably invented that story."

"What do you mean?"

"I'm afraid to say that cops sometimes say stuff like that."

I frowned. "You mean they make it up? Invent the whole thing?"

Blake nodded solemnly. "Yes, to see if the person will admit to it, or at least to gauge their reaction."

I thought it over. "Well, if it *is* true, then the person who gave them the tip off is the murderer—what other reason would a person have to lie like that?"

"I'll try to find out if there really was a tip-off."

"Thanks." I fell into silence and stared blankly into the fire. I had wanted it to be a romantic dinner, but it hadn't worked that way at all. I was miserable and feeling sorry for myself.

CHAPTER 12

"Oh, Sibyl, it's obvious!" Mr Buttons called out to me as he returned with a platter of cucumber sandwiches and tea. He set the meal in front of me—crusts cut off, as was his tradition—and sat down, taking a long, slow sip from his tea.

"What's obvious, Mr Buttons?" I asked, opting to wait until I'd heard him out before grabbing a bite to eat. There was nothing worse than trying to have a conversation with a mouthful of food.

"The murderer! We both know who it was," Mr Buttons exclaimed between large bites of his sandwich. He leant in closely and spoke in little more than a whisper. "It was Dorothy. I bet she was the one who saw you buying the antifreeze and told the police in order to throw suspicion off herself. She's the murderer, you mark my words."

I sighed audibly and leant back in my chair. "You say this about everything, Mr Buttons. Quite literally everything. The other day you blamed her for that time you got lost on your way out of town, despite the fact that it happened about a year before you'd actually met her. You even blame her whenever the weather turns bad."

"It's nature's way of defending itself against her," he remarked quite seriously. I drank some of my tea and took a sandwich of my own, deciding it would be best not to argue. Dorothy was certainly hard to get along with, but that was no reason to accuse her of murder, especially when there was no evidence that she was involved. I'd normally take Mr Buttons' words to heart, but it was easy to tell he was being more than a little silly.

"Imagine, Mr Buttons, if it wasn't Dorothy. Hypothetically, if it had been somebody else, who seems likely to you?" I asked, hoping my ploy wasn't too obvious.

Luckily, it seemed to have worked. Mr Buttons leant on the table and stroked his chin, clearly thinking. "Well, we know it wasn't us, since we weren't at the house when it all happened. And unless Cressida has taken her art to a horrible new level, we can count her out, too. Even if it wasn't completely out of character for her, she not only doesn't have a motive, but would be actively hurting her business if she murdered somebody here." Mr Buttons took another sip of his tea and picked up another sandwich. "I suppose the guests are the most likely, given that any one of them could have found out that you had invited Sally to your cottage. What about Prudence?"

I nodded. "I think that's a good start, yes. She's not especially suspicious, I suppose, but then murderers rarely are."

"But what motive would she have?" Mr Buttons asked. "They seemed more than a little friendly at dinner."

"Exactly," I said pointedly. "Roland was married, so it's possible that he rejected Prudence in favour of Sally."

"I admit to not knowing the poor man very well, but it strikes me that he wasn't the most loyal person," Mr Buttons said sadly. "Are you sure that's a good motive?"

"I don't think a good motive for murder truly exists, Mr Buttons," I said, taking a sandwich for myself. "But I do think it's a possibility worth investigating. It's a great idea of yours that we talk to some people at Prudence's lecture today. It might end up revealing something we've missed."

Mr Buttons thought for at least a full minute before replying. "Yes, I suppose." He sighed long and hard. "If only to prove that she's not at fault so we can get back to investigating Dorothy. I'm ready whenever you are."

Mr Buttons and I left almost immediately, driving directly to the university to catch the lecture. We wanted to make sure that we arrived before it finished so we could talk to people who knew Prudence before they left. Unfortunately, we'd decided to leave around lunch time, so traffic was unusually heavy. Of course, 'unusually heavy' traffic in Pharmidale amounted to only a handful of extra cars, so we still made it there in decent time.

As the town's main—some would say only—attraction, the university was large, and was comprised of many large buildings over one hundred and fifty acres. We parked outside the Arts building and hurried up the hill and then into the building in the direction of the A4 lecture hall, hoping we weren't too late.

As we entered, I immediately wondered if we'd found the wrong room. There was a large, cheering crowd, and the sound of laughter echoed through the hall. As we continued down the aisle, we were greeted with the sight of Prudence standing before a brick wall, onto which various images of spotted quolls were being projected.

There was a large crowd of students sitting in rows of seats along the hall. All of them seemed to be completely enraptured in the conversation, not at all like any student I'd ever known. Each was so invested in the lecture that not a single one turned to look as we entered the room.

It wasn't long before I noticed that Mr Buttons was also intently staring at the screen. I raised my eyebrows, wondering what had him so interested. All the screen showed were several spotted quolls, and while Prudence was lecturing in an extremely animated way, motioning to the different ways quolls moved and acted, it didn't seem like something Mr Buttons would be interested in.

Before I could react, he ran straight past me and directly onto the stage. Prudence turned to look at him, stopping her lecture with a stunned expression. Mr Buttons ran straight past her and pulled a napkin out of his jacket pocket, using it to rub a tiny spot off the wall onto which the images were being projected. He calmly walked back off the stage, giving Prudence a small polite nod as he passed her.

I didn't think Mr Buttons could do anything more embarrassing until he licked his finger and rubbed a small piece of food off the cheek of some poor student sitting in the front row. I clasped my hands over my face to hide it as Prudence slowly cleared her throat and resumed the lecture.

The lecture continued, but try as I might, there was simply no way I could pay attention. I didn't think I'd ever heard anything as boring before in my life. Prudence was halfway through describing the typical ecologies of the spotted quoll—also known as the 'Tiger Quoll' as I'd just learned—when Mr Buttons turned to me and spoke in a hushed whisper.

"This is dreadfully dull, Sibyl," he said, glancing over at the stage. "Can we just go and do something else until it's over? I think we passed some paint that was drying that we could watch."

I nudged Mr Buttons in the ribs to make him

quiet. "We can't just leave, because something important might come up. If she talks about her life even a little, it might give us some insight. Just be patient."

Almost immediately, I regretted being so adamant. We sat there for what felt like several more hours, though realistically probably wasn't even a full fifty minutes. While we learned plenty about the quoll's natural habitat and eating habits, we didn't learn a thing about Prudence, much less any signs of a motive. Finally, Prudence said that tea and coffee were to be served in the staff room, and I didn't think I'd heard sweeter words in my life. Mr Buttons and I all but sprinted to the room and made ourselves some coffee, desperately trying to chase away the exhaustion of having listened to that entire lecture.

"Goodness gracious, Sibyl," Mr Buttons said, rubbing his eyes. "I wish we hadn't done that. We didn't even learn anything useful."

I sighed, grabbing the most delicious looking cookie I could, then deciding that I might as well take a few more. "I know, I know, I'm sorry. Still, let's talk to people here who know Prudence." I motioned to the large crowd that was slowly pouring into the room.

"We're not going to find a motive, Sibyl," Mr Buttons said, lowering his voice. "Unless Prudence broke into your house to give Roland a lecture on quolls so he'd kill himself, I don't think she's responsible."

"I know you think it's Dorothy, Mr Buttons, but we have to ask around at least."

Mr Buttons sighed as well, but nodded to me, indicating that he at least agreed on some level.

"Hello, Mr Buttons," Prudence said with a smile. "Hi, Sibyl, I didn't know you were in attendance today. I hope you enjoyed the lecture."

"Oh, yes, it was very interesting," I lied, resisting the urge to run away in case she started talking about quolls again.

"Well, I'm glad you enjoyed it," Prudence said with a smile. "If you'll excuse me, some people have been clamouring for answers to their questions. I'll talk to you both back at the boarding house later on." She nodded and walked into a large crowd of people who were indeed vying for her attention.

"Let's ask around," I said to Mr Buttons, who looked as if he was about to cry. "I know there'll be more quoll talk, but if it starts heading in that direction, just bail out of the conversation."

"How, Sibyl?" Mr Buttons asked. "I'm never any good at these things. If I try to excuse myself mid-conversation, I always invent some embarrassing excuse that doesn't even make sense."

"Oh, Mr Buttons, you're being silly," I said, putting my hands on my hips. "Go try it on that guy." I indicated a man who was standing alone, slowly pouring himself a coffee. "Just ask him what he thinks of Prudence. If he starts to talk about quolls, just make up some normal excuse and come back here. You'll be fine."

Mr Buttons sighed and rubbed his temples, but agreed to try. I walked slightly closer to overhear the conversation.

Mr Buttons greeted the man cheerfully. "Hello, do you know Professor Prudence Paget very well?" he asked, clearly not one to beat around the bush. It took less than a minute before the conversation devolved entirely into the stranger excitedly talking about the nominate subspecies of quoll that can be found in the wet forests of south eastern Australia and Tasmania. I thought about coming to Mr Buttons' rescue, but decided he'd need to learn how to do it himself or he'd never figure it out.

Instead, I opted to ask around for myself.

Prudence was busy talking to several people, so I figured it would be safe to ask about her elsewhere in the room. Unfortunately, my experience was similar to Mr Buttons,' and everybody I spoke to seemed to be far more interested in quolls than Prudence, and several times I found myself resisting the urge to explain that I found *anything* more interesting than quolls, before excusing myself.

Mr Buttons and I eventually rendezvoused at the snack table, each of us more exhausted than before. "How did you go?" Mr Buttons asked me, sounding like he'd just run a marathon.

"Not well," I admitted, taking another cookie. "Nobody cared about Prudence, much less had anything useful on her."

"Well, we're lucky that I'm such a natural conversationalist," Mr Buttons said with a smile. "Apparently, Prudence applied for a very large grant some years ago. I do mean a *very* large grant, Sibyl, to the tune of hundreds of thousands of dollars. Those grants were called *ARC Large Grants*, back in the day. It was going well until it was knocked back by the grants committee, a committee headed by none other than Roland Cavendish himself."

I raised my eyebrows, and Mr Buttons nodded at me. "That's a good reason for her to hate him, but why was she so friendly with him at dinner? Was that just a ruse?"

Mr Buttons shrugged at me, and I felt every bit as lost. What did it mean?

CHAPTER 13

I watched as yet another piece of baby spinach flew off my plate and landed on Mr Buttons' plate. I had long since given up trying to catch them. Perhaps I shouldn't have ordered the pumpkin salad, because the green bits were hard to hold down in the gale force wind.

Mr Buttons, on the other hand, had ordered two wraps, and those were in no danger of leaving his plate.

"Why do we have to sit outside in this freezing weather?" I asked him. "It's blowing a gale. No one else is out here, if you hadn't noticed."

Mr Buttons leant across the table and addressed me in a conspiratorial tone. "Exactly. I don't want anyone to overhear what I say."

I looked around me once more. I had chosen a table without an umbrella, quite wisely on my part, because the umbrellas at the other tables, despite being shut, looked in immediate danger of becoming airborne. I could see the other patrons all sitting inside, no doubt enjoying the warmth of the open fire. I was just about to insist that we go inside, when a young couple walked out and took a seat at a nearby table. They tried to open one of the umbrellas, but before they managed to do so, a waitress sprinted down the pathway towards them.

"Oh my goodness, what on earth do you think you're doing?" she snapped at them.

"Can we put one of the umbrellas up?" the man asked her.

"Of course not!" she said in a raised voice. "That would be a really stupid idea!" She hurried to shut the umbrella, which was already lifting itself into the air, borne by the violent wind. The couple hurried away to another table.

The waitress pulled the umbrella out of its holder and threw it to the ground, then stormed off in a huff. "She's a cranky one," Mr Buttons said.

I tried to part my hair, which was violently

flying around my face, to look at Mr Buttons, when another piece of baby spinach flew from my plate and landed in his hair. "I think I'll get frostbite, maybe even hypothermia, if we stay out here," I said as a hint.

Mr Buttons remained oblivious to my pleading. "Sibyl, I had a revelation last night, as I was lying in my bed and watching fly spots on the ceiling, wondering how soon I could remove them." I sighed, but he pressed on. "You know, I have no idea why it didn't occur to me before." He paused for dramatic effect.

"What do you mean? The fly spots?"

Mr Buttons looked disappointed. "No, Sibyl. James, James the ghost hunter. Remember him?"

"Of course I remember him," I said. "He *did* try to push me out a window."

Mr Buttons shrugged. "James is Dorothy's nephew, so of course he'll know any dirt on the awful woman. He'll know if there's a connection between Dorothy and the vic!"

Not Dorothy again, I thought. Aloud I said, "I thought we suspected Prudence Paget now? Remember how we said it was suspicious that Roland ruined her academic career, but she was so nice to him at dinner?" I put my napkin over the last piece of my baby spinach to hold it down. "Anyway, do you actually think James would talk to us?"

"He's a captive audience, so to speak," Mr Buttons said with a giggle, just before a napkin blew into his head. "He's in jail. We'll go and visit him, and take bribes."

"Bribes?" I pulled a face. "Do you mean a chocolate cake with a file in the middle of it?"

Mr Buttons ignored my facetious remark, and leant down to fetch papers from his briefcase. He put a stack of papers in front of me and handed me a pen, but at that point, an even more violent gust of wind appeared and blew the papers all over the seating area.

It took us both a good five minutes to retrieve all the paperwork. Well, I had retrieved most of the papers, and when I finished, I looked up to see Mr Buttons looking distastefully at a muddy piece of paper.

"We need to go inside," I said firmly. "Otherwise, all these papers will get dirty." That did the trick. Mr Buttons was happy to follow me inside, where we were lucky enough to get a seat that had just been vacated, right by the fire. The two people who were on their way to the same table shot us nasty glances.

Mr Buttons daintily dabbed at the mud spots on his piece of paper with a napkin. "Don't speak too loudly," he warned me. "You know what the locals are like."

I looked around me, to see all pairs of eyes on us. I had grown so accustomed to living in a small country town that I no longer noticed the attention that the locals paid each other. In the city, no one gave each other a second glance, no matter how they were acting or how strangely they were dressed. Yet here in the country, everyone stared at everyone else. It reminded me of the time that Mr Buttons had taken me for a walk in a different direction, down a laneway between two paddocks filled with cows. The cows came to the fence and stared at us intently. It seems that both people and animals in small country towns were fascinated by other creatures.

I moved my chair closer to the warmth and the comfort of the fire. I love the smell of burning wood, and half thought that I should ask them who their wood man was so I could suggest him to Cressida. This wood was clearly nice and old, whereas Cressida's hadn't been dried sufficiently. I suppressed a giggle, figuring I was becoming quite the country girl now, knowledgeable about weather patterns and wood.

I looked up to see that Mr Buttons seemed to have rearranged the papers to his satisfaction, although he was clearly displeased with the muddy corners. "You haven't told me what all this is for," I said.

"It's the paperwork that we have to submit to visit James in jail," he said. "We need to submit it quickly, because it takes ages to process."

I was dismayed. "Ages?" I repeated. "Those detectives will have *me* in jail by then, and that's even supposing James *does* know something, and that's assuming that Dorothy *is* the killer."

Mr Buttons smiled. "A journey of one thousand miles begins with the first step." He waved his hand at me. "We don't have a Tardis, so this is the best we can do."

I had to agree. "Can we pay a rush fee or anything?"

Mr Buttons simply looked at me over his glasses by way of response.

"While we're here, in the warmth, can we go through the other suspects please, Mr Buttons?"

Mr Buttons narrowed his eyes, but then nodded somewhat reluctantly.

"His wife, Sally, is a likely suspect," I said. "I did see her with that man. Then again, the motive could have been jealousy. He was an obvious flirt."

"So are a lot of men," Mr Buttons pointed out, "and their wives don't kill them."

"Sally and Roland had no children, and there was the money."

Mr Buttons shook his head. "The vic wasn't a millionaire. He just had a salary, a good salary at that, but that wasn't enough financial motive for someone to murder him."

"Well, she'll get the whole house and it might be worth quite a bit."

Mr Buttons continued to shake his head. "No millions are involved, and that's not enough to murder someone for money. Besides, she could just have divorced him if she wanted to get out of the marriage."

"Maybe he was so irritating that she didn't want to go through a divorce," I said. "Divorce is very stressful and expensive. I'm speaking from experience, mind you."

At that moment, the fire popped and a piece

of coal flew onto the floor near Mr Buttons' foot. He gasped, picked it up in a napkin, and threw both napkin and coal into the fire in one skilled movement.

I could see him eyeing off the blackened fire grate, and was afraid he would create a scene by scrubbing off the soot, so I tried to divert his attention. "I have to say, Prudence is now the top of my list, after what we found out about her at the seminar."

Thankfully, Mr Buttons left the soot alone and sat back on his chair. "You know, I was beginning to think it was Prudence Paget too, but after thinking about it all night, I'm now convinced it's Dorothy."

I resisted the urge to roll my eyes. "Mr Buttons, Prudence has a motive. You heard yourself how Roland knocked her back for a big research grant, and that impacted her career badly. That would have to make someone awfully resentful, especially a career academic like Prudence."

Mr Buttons frowned. "I don't really see how that's a motive for murder, Sibyl. By all accounts, it happened years ago. If she was going to murder him, she would've murdered him back then."

"Most likely she hasn't seen him again for years," I said. "Perhaps she didn't have the opportunity, and something could have set her off. After all, you have to admit that it was suspicious how she was flirting so outrageously with him, given that she surely couldn't have liked the man."

Mr Buttons' eyebrows shot up and down several times in succession. "Yes, I do find it suspicious, but like I said, it was a long time ago. Maybe she's moved on and just let bygones be bygones. Haven't you ever been outwardly friendly with someone that you didn't actually like?"

I thought it over for a moment. He did have a point.

"We didn't really discuss it in the car on the way home yesterday," I said. Every time I had tried to bring it up, Mr Buttons had changed the subject, saying that Dorothy had a guilty face because her eyebrows were asymmetrical, or some such other ridiculous excuse. "I mean, who else could it be?" I silently berated myself for saying such a thing. I knew full well what his answer would be. I pushed on. "You know, it surely has to be Prudence. She *does* have a motive. She lost hundreds of thousands of dollars of funding, and she is a career academic after all. Academia is highly competitive, and I'm sure people have been killed for less."

Mr Buttons pursed his lips. "Someone murdered Roland with antifreeze, and tried to set me up to take the fall for the murder," I added. "Someone tipped off the police with the false claim that I was having an affair with Roland, and that I had been seen in town buying antifreeze. What's more, they murdered him in my house! Whoever the murderer is, they are doing their best to frame me. It has to be Prudence, or my second choice is Sally."

Mr Buttons waved a hand in disagreement. I watched as he opened his mouth, and I thought that if he said the word 'Dorothy' again, I would scream and run out of the café.

My worst fears were realised. "Dorothy," he began, but before he could continue, the local postman hurried over to the table.

"Haven't you heard the news?" he asked us.

"What news?" I said.

"I thought you hadn't heard the news because you're both sitting here so calmly," he said, smirking.

"Please tell us what's happened, if you would be so kind," Mr Buttons said.

"It's your cook, Dorothy," the postman said. "Haven't you heard? The police found her DNA on that threatening letter!"

CHAPTER 14

"There is the detectives' vehicle," Mr Buttons said, somewhat unnecessarily. Sure enough, the vehicle was parked directly outside the boarding house. "I had hoped to see Dorothy being dragged away in handcuffs by the time we arrived," he added in a disappointed tone.

"Let's get inside as fast as we can," I said. "I want to know what's going on as soon as possible."

The very second Mr Buttons opened the main door to the boarding house, we heard the sound of pots and pans being flung around in the kitchen. We exchanged glances, and then hurried in that direction. I was about to go in, when Mr

Buttons restrained me. He put his finger to his mouth and indicated that we should listen in. It was no hard task, given that Dorothy was screaming and the detectives had raised their voices.

"I tell you, it was that man at the post office. He was obviously trying to frame me for the murder, but of course I didn't know that at the time!" I heard Dorothy slam down a pot for emphasis.

"So, your story is that you were walking up the steps to the post office when a man approached you and asked you to seal the letter for him and post it." Detective Roberts' voice held a good measure of disbelief.

"Yes, he said he'd had just had an emergency call, that his mother had taken ill, and he had to race her to the hospital," Dorothy said.

"And why didn't you tell us this before?" Roberts asked her.

"I had no idea that the letter I posted for him was a threatening letter," she said loudly.

"You didn't look at the letter?" Henderson asked her.

"No, I'm not a busybody. Are you trying to say I'm a busybody?" Her words were punctuated by the sound of another pot banging.

"And what did this man look like?" Roberts asked her.

"I've already told you a hundred times," Dorothy yelled. "Are you trying to trick me? He looked like someone I've seen at Sibyl's house."

Mr Buttons and I exchanged glances. I was furious. Perhaps Mr Buttons had been right about Dorothy being the murderer after all.

"Are you sure?" Roberts asked her.

"No," Dorothy snapped. "My eyesight is not good, and my memory is not much better. It's just that when I saw him, I thought he looked like a friend of Sibyl's. That's all."

"We need you to accompany us to the station to make a statement," Roberts said.

More pots banged, and Mr Buttons and I took that as our cue to leave. We hurried back down the corridor and into the sitting room, where we peeped around the door and saw Dorothy preceding the two detectives out the front door.

I turned to Mr Buttons, but before I could say anything, Cressida burst into the room. "Why have the police taken Dorothy away?"

I hurried to speak before Mr Buttons had the

opportunity. "Her DNA was found on the threatening letter, but she says that a man gave it to her to post."

"Why would someone do that?" Cressida asked.

Mr Buttons snorted rudely. "Exactly!"

"She said he was in a hurry to leave because he'd just received an emergency phone call, so he handed it to her and asked her to post it," I explained.

"Oh yes, that makes sense," Cressida said.

"It makes sense?" Mr Buttons repeated. "My dear woman, it makes not a modicum of sense at all. Dorothy is obviously the culprit, and what's more, she tried to implicate Sibyl."

Cressida turned to me. "She did?"

"She said that the man looked like a friend of mine," I said.

Cressida frowned so deeply that little pieces of her makeup cracked and fell off. "What friend?"

"Exactly!" Mr Buttons said. "Dorothy is the murderer, and she tried to implicate Sibyl to the police just then. We know that the murderer has tried to frame Sibyl. First of all, the murderer murdered the poor man in Sibyl's house, and then she told the police that Sibyl was having an affair with him, and then she told the police that Sibyl bought antifreeze. Now, Dorothy has told the police that the man who posted the letter looks like a friend of Sibyl's. Case closed!" he concluded with a triumphant note.

"Lord Farringdon says things are not as they seem." Cressida stooped down to stroke the cat's long fur.

"Now that we know Dorothy's safely out of the way and has no chance of returning in the next few minutes," Mr Buttons said, "this gives us a good opportunity to search the kitchen for antifreeze."

I shook my head. "Even if Dorothy is the murderer, she wouldn't be silly enough to keep antifreeze in the kitchen. She probably keeps it in her car."

Mr Buttons beamed. "So you *do* think that Dorothy's the murderer now?"

I rubbed my forehead. I had the beginnings of a headache. "No, I don't think Dorothy is the murderer, but I was speaking hypothetically. People don't keep antifreeze in their kitchen, they keep it in their car or near their car. Besides, every person in town would have antifreeze."

Cressida agreed. "No one in their right mind

would leave antifreeze out of their cars in this weather. But didn't they put a bittering agent in antifreeze to make it bitter about ten or so years ago?" she asked. "I saw a documentary on Australian murders recently, and it said that people stopped using it to murder people once they put the bittering agent in."

"Yes, I googled it," Mr Buttons said. "Though the reason they used the bittering agent was so that children and pets wouldn't eat it, because it tastes quite sweet without the agent. I also discovered that it takes about a quarter of a cup to kill someone. It's lucky that the vic had that medical condition, hypogeusia, leaving him unable to taste food properly."

"Lucky?" I echoed. "If he didn't have that condition, he'd probably be alive now."

"I meant lucky for Dorothy," Mr Buttons explained patiently.

"His wife of course knew about his condition," I pointed out. "And so did Prudence, as he told all of us about it."

Mr Buttons nodded sagely. "And so did Dorothy. She was right there when he mentioned it to everyone. And it was a chocolate mint sundae you said you saw next to the body, Sibyl, was it not? That would explain away the green colour. What type of sundae did you intend to give Sally, Sibyl?"

I shrugged. "Just normal chocolate, I suppose," I said. "To be honest, Mr Buttons, I hadn't really considered the intricacies of the sundae that had yet to exist."

"Well, that says as much as if you'd planned a mint sundae," Mr Buttons announced triumphantly, and I was beginning to think that he was losing his grasp on his deduction. "That meant that the victim, Roland, didn't know what kind of sundae to expect. So he wouldn't have been suspicious about a mint sundae."

"Wait, wait," I said, pinching the bridge of my nose. "What exactly do you think happened? Do you think Dorothy wore a wig and pretended to be me and served him a sundae? Do you think she broke in and left the sundae on the table, and that Roland just ate a strange green sundae he found? Roland wasn't even the one I invited over for a sundae. This still leaves a whole lot unexplained."

"Well," Mr Buttons began, scratching his chin. "It's easy to see that Dorothy could have gotten into your cottage. After all, she has a key to every room in the boarding house, as well as your cottage. Besides, you never lock it—anyone could have walked in. It's entirely possible that she left a note for Roland that said to meet you in the cottage. The note could have also said that the sundae inside was for him."

I sighed. "This is a bit of a stretch, Mr Buttons. What would the note have said? 'Hello Roland, meet me in the cottage and eat the first green thing you see. Sincerely, your secret admirer'?" I asked sarcastically. Dorothy was certainly suspicious, but it was hard to believe that she was the murderer based on such flimsy evidence.

Cressida suddenly spoke up. "I've got it! Maybe the real murderer gave her the note to give to Roland, which is why her DNA was on it!"

Mr Buttons and I sighed in unison, though I spoke first. "Cressida, Dorothy's DNA was found on the threatening letter. We're talking about a note that probably doesn't exist. We're just throwing around hypothetical situations to figure out what happened."

"Oh," Cressida said, somewhat deflated. "Well, why do you think your friend was sending the threatening letter?"

"I don't have any friends!" I said dramatically. "I mean, wait, no. I do have friends, but none who send threatening letters. Dorothy is either confused or trying to implicate me for it."

"Which proves that she's the murderer, since we know that you don't have any friends who would send the letter," Mr Buttons chimed in, looking quite smug.

"We don't know that for sure," I continued, undeterred. "We just know that she's saying someone gave her the letter and that she thought he was a friend of mine. She could be genuinely confused, but maybe she's just trying to push it off on to me because she's scared, whether or not she's actually guilty. Or, she could even just be using the opportunity to get me in some trouble, since we know she's not my biggest fan."

"We should tell the police that she's lying," Mr Buttons said sternly.

I shook my head again. "What would that do? We can't actually prove anything, and neither can she. It's all hearsay either way. Honestly, at this point I think that actively denying her claims to the police might make us seem even more suspicious. If she's guilty, the police should figure it out." I hoped to get Mr Buttons off the topic of Dorothy's guilt for once. He'd say she faked the moon landing if he could figure out a way to implicate her. "Besides, the police can't arrest me until they find proof. And as we all know, no evidence of my guilt actually exists, because I'm innocent," I said, swallowing nervously. While what I had said was ostensibly true, I wasn't quite so confident that I wouldn't be arrested. All the police would really need was something that appeared to be evidence, even if it was unrelated. It had been my experience that some police officers weren't too worried about the specifics of law if it meant catching somebody who they thought was a murderer.

Besides, even going to court could be a disaster, whether or not I was convicted. If I were dragged into a court to prove my innocence, it would cause all sorts of other issues, such as huge legal fees, time away from work, and garnering a bad reputation. None of those were things I wanted to go through, much less the chance of going to jail for a crime with which I had no involvement.

"I suppose you're right," Mr Buttons admitted softly. "Well, we can investigate other suspects if it makes you feel better. Besides, it's the fastest way to cross them off the list, since Dorothy is the only murderer."

"The *only* murderer?" I asked, thinking. What if there really had been more than one? It was possible that the threatening letter was written by somebody who wasn't the murderer. That could possibly implicate Dorothy, though I still very much doubted that she was guilty. There wasn't much to love about the woman, but murder seemed to be well and truly out of her league, even if verbal abuse wasn't. I sighed, realising that discovering the identity of a single murderer was hard enough without considering the existence of another. Besides, it didn't really change the process, since we still needed some kind of evidence.

"We need to find something that gives us a clue to the murderer's identity," I said aloud, hoping that Mr Buttons wouldn't bring up Dorothy again. To my relief, he simply nodded, and Cressida busied herself by patting Lord Farringdon.

CHAPTER 15

The first thing I noticed was how thin she was. The word that came to mind was 'skeletal,' because she did indeed resemble a skeleton, at least, one that was covered in too much makeup and designer clothing. She was tall to the point of being intimidating despite her otherwise small frame, and it was immediately clear that she was wealthy. Or at least, she had been when she had purchased her clothes and jewellery, but it was entirely possible that she'd spent her life savings on those.

She had long black hair, which stood in stark contrast to her pale white skin and incredibly bright red lipstick. I couldn't help but wonder why somebody would make themselves look like that on purpose, though she certainly seemed to have the confidence to pull it off. Speaking of pulling it off, her long, clearly false eyelashes were constantly on the edge of escaping her face.

I was a bit too far away to hear what was happening, but the woman was talking to Cressida at the counter, so I assumed that she was checking into the boarding house. I always tried not to judge people based on their appearance, but this woman seemed to be undeniably stuck up, as during the entire conversation she held her chin high, as though she were literally looking down her nose at Cressida.

Cressida was doing her best to remain polite, but having known her for so long it was obvious that she was uncomfortable. Still, I found watching the two of them talk to be quite funny. Both of them had a penchant for extremely strange make up, and I briefly wondered what a stranger would think if they saw them here. They'd surely think that they'd accidentally stumbled into some kind of strange clown hotel.

"Hello," I said, smiling as I approached the counter. Cressida smiled back, and the woman turned to face me, nose still held high. I considered that seeing directly up somebody's nostrils was one of the least elegant ways you could be introduced to them. "I'm Sibyl. I live out the back," I explained, though I immediately realised that made me sound like I was squatting behind the boarding house.

"Florence," the woman replied simply, before turning back to Cressida. Her voice was nasal and irritating. "Are we all done here?"

"Yes, we are. Let me show you to your room," Cressida said with a strained smile.

"No need," Florence said with what seemed to be a small sigh. "This place is awfully small. I'm sure I can find it myself."

As she spoke, Florence drew a long, black stick from her purse and placed a cigarette in the end of it. She calmly lit it and drew a long, deep breath, before exhaling the smoke, idly watching as it drifted further into the boarding house.

"I'm afraid we have a no smoking policy, dear," Cressida informed her politely, though Florence took no notice whatsoever, and blew rings of smoke into Cressida's face.

I shrugged at Cressida, who appeared to be quite distressed and at a loss as to what to do. I personally found it quite annoying. Florence didn't at all give a good first impression. Florence wandered further into the boarding house, presumably hunting for her room.

"Who was that?" I asked Cressida, hoping to gain some insight into why Cressida was treating her so nicely despite her rudeness.

"Florence," Cressida said simply, as though it were a perfectly normal explanation. "She's here to board for a little while."

"But she was so rude!" I said perhaps a little too loudly, lowering my voice before I spoke again in case Florence heard me. "Why did you let her act like that?"

"Well, Sibyl, she's a paying customer. That's all it really is," Cressida explained sadly. "This boarding house has had one too many murders to turn away paying customers willy nilly."

I felt for Cressida. There had been an unusual number of murders in the boarding house, though I supposed that even one murder was an unusual amount.

"Hello," Mr Buttons said, announcing his arrival. "How are we today?"

"Not great," I said honestly. "The rudest guest just arrived, but Cressida's in a tough position, so she can't say anything."

"Oh, Cressida," Mr Buttons said, putting his

hand on her shoulder. "You need to start being more strict with people. Especially Dorothy."

"Oh, enough of that!" Cressida gently slapped away Mr Buttons' hand. "You just want Dorothy gone."

"No!" Mr Buttons sounded offended. "Well, yes. But I also want you to be happy. This boarding house deserves to be successful."

"I'm happy, I promise." Cressida smiled. "With the success of my art, profit from the boarding house is less essential than ever. Though I would like to have fewer murders here. None would be ideal."

We all sighed collectively. "Well, if money's not an issue, why are you putting up with her?" I asked again.

"It's professionalism, Sibyl," Cressida explained. "I don't want to generate a reputation as a boarding house that rejects guests, especially after what happened to poor Roland. So it isn't her money so much as the business that I need, if that makes sense."

I nodded, though I didn't quite agree. Florence struck me as the type who would either complain about her lodgings or just wouldn't bring them up at all.

"Well, I'm yet to meet the woman, but judging from your tone, she sounds like bad news," Mr Buttons said, nodding sternly. "We don't need more bad news, that much is certain."

"You might be right," Cressida said softly. "But let's give her a chance. Maybe she's just been having a bad day, or something."

"Sibyl, why don't you come to dinner tonight with all the guests?" Mr Buttons suggested. "It will be a good way to learn more about the new arrival, and who knows, maybe we'll turn out to get along just fine."

I readily agreed. I also wanted to have another conversation with Sally. She was now my prime suspect, which made confronting her in private quite nerve-wracking. A dinner sounded like the perfect way to try to dig up more information about her, or to catch her in an incriminating lie.

I decided to spend the rest of the day at home, alternating between trying to relax and thinking about the case. Being at home in the cold cottage was unpleasant, and even more so, given the fact that Roland had died there, but at the same time it felt like nothing was different about it. Maybe that was the strangest thing—despite the fact that a man had died in my house, it felt exactly the same.

Just before nightfall, we all met in the dining room. There was myself, Mr Buttons, Cressida, Florence, and Sally. I was pleased to see that Sally had come, as my whole plan would have been a disaster if she had been otherwise engaged.

I thought about asking why Prudence hadn't come, but decided it might be a bit of a sore point for Sally after seeing her flirt with Roland. Besides, Prudence was probably just busy with her quoll work. I also wasn't sure if Mr Buttons or I could handle any more information about quolls.

Florence seemed more talkative than I had initially assumed, although she still wasn't especially friendly. We all spoke for a little while over dinner, typical small talk with no real meaning. I didn't like feeling so manipulative, but I just wanted to try to talk to Sally to fish for clues, so all of this small talk was frustrating me.

Suddenly, Mr Buttons jumped out of his chair and ran to the kitchen door. The rest of us sat in stunned silence, waiting for several seconds as loud banging sounds echoed through the building. About a minute later, he sprinted back into the room with a can of fly spray. Instead of explaining what was happening to anybody present, he instead opted simply to spray Florence's dress.

Florence screamed wildly and jumped to her feet, knocking her chair to the floor and brushing the spray off herself.

While Florence struck me as the kind of person who would overreact to simple issues, this seemed a fair reaction. I noticed that one of her fake eyelashes had floated to the floor.

"What are you doing?" she screamed, blinking furiously.

"There was an enormous fly on your face, and it was an eyesore," Mr Buttons said calmly. "It fell onto your dress and so I took care of it for you." He slowly walked back to the kitchen.

I looked at the fake eyelash on the ground and sighed audibly. I wasn't sure if Mr Buttons had mistaken it for a fly, or if he simply didn't like Florence much. Either way, it was hard not to find it quite amusing.

I fully expected Florence to scream in Mr Buttons' face, but to my surprise she managed to remain quite diplomatic about the whole thing— that is, once she had returned from the bathroom, inexplicably with new fake eyelashes. Before too much longer, we had returned to eating in relative peace, though Florence took to flinching every time Mr Buttons made a sudden move. That was probably wise.

"So, what brings you here, Florence?" I asked, trying to get the conversation flowing. I really just wanted to talk to Sally, but I couldn't think of a good way to start a conversation with her.

"My boyfriend, Roland, was recently killed here," she replied simply. An awful silence fell over the room, and I briefly considered simply running away. It wasn't the best or most dignified response to an awkward social situation, but it would have been an effective way to remove myself from it.

We all looked at Sally, who was wearing an expression that sat somewhere between horrified and enraged. All of a sudden, she launched herself from her chair across the table, diving at Florence. Dishes and food flew everywhere. Mr Buttons, Cressida, and I stood up and backed away from the pair.

"Oh, dear," Cressida said, putting her hand to her mouth. "I can't believe Lord Farringdon didn't tell me who she was." Lord Farringdon sprinted from the room by way of response.

I realised we should help somehow, but the three of us were in complete shock. Sally had Florence by the hair and was pulling as hard as she could, before Florence did some kind of judo throw and pulled Sally's hair. I was worried that getting close would result in severe injury. Still, the fighting didn't seem like it was going to cause any permanent harm. At least, I hoped it wouldn't.

What really surprised me was Sally's reaction. Up until that point, I had been convinced that she had been the one to kill Roland, but now it seemed like she had really loved him. Was I wrong? It was possible that she was simply acting enraged, but as I dodged a chair that flew through the room, that felt more unlikely than ever.

It was also possible that Sally was angry with Florence for something else, but she hadn't become angry until Florence had revealed that she was Roland's mistress. I nimbly ducked a plate, breaking my concentration in the process. I'd have to figure this out after we'd stopped them from killing each other, or at least balding each other. Thank goodness Dorothy hadn't entered the fray.

Mr Buttons and I managed to drag them apart after a great deal of effort, and then they both returned to their rooms in private. I felt responsible for the whole fight, given that I had asked the question that had started it all, despite the fact I knew it hadn't truly been my fault. I sighed and rubbed my temples. This was all too much. I needed some sleep.

CHAPTER 16

"Why would Florence just come out and announce that she was his mistress?"

Mr Buttons shrugged. "And didn't you say you saw Sally with a man? If she herself had a lover, then why would she object to her husband having one?"

"I thought about it all last night," I admitted, "and I didn't come up with anything useful."

"It certainly was a strange dinner," Mr Buttons said. "Anyway, has she gone yet?"

I looked around the corner to check, saw that Dorothy was still in the kitchen, and ducked back to safety. "She's still here," I hissed, hoping desperately that Dorothy couldn't hear us.

"But we heard her say she was going to town!" Mr Buttons said far too loudly, again displaying that he had no sense of volume. "What do we do if she's changed her mind?"

I shrugged at him. "Mr Buttons, I don't know what you want me to do as it is, much less if she changes her mind. Do you have something planned?"

Before he could reply, Dorothy marched loudly out of the kitchen, muttering to herself. Mr Buttons and I followed her as carefully as we could, all the way to the front door, to make sure she had actually left. Sure enough, we saw her car fly down the driveway and away from the boarding house.

Mr Buttons practically cheered, though he still looked strangely nervous about something. "What is it?" I asked impatiently. "Why were you so eager for her to leave? More than usual, I mean."

"It's our chance!" he explained unhelpfully. "We can check the shed behind the kitchen for antifreeze. If she has some, it will prove her guilt, surely."

"Mr Buttons, everybody has antifreeze," I explained with a sigh. "I do mean everybody. It's hard to live in such a cold town without it. We've been over this a thousand times already."

"All the same, we should explore. There might be a clue of some kind. Surely you won't turn down a good chance to find evidence, Sibyl?"

I sighed again, pinching the bridge of my nose. "All right, okay, fine. You win. Let's go have a look, but quickly," I said nervously, realising that we had no idea how long Dorothy was going to be away. She could be gone for hours, or be back any minute. Either way, we had to hurry.

As Mr Buttons and I walked to the garden shed, I couldn't help but feel it was a terrible idea. It all felt so rushed, and there was no way Dorothy would leave any kind of evidence somewhere so accessible. At the same time, I didn't want to disappoint Mr Buttons, and if Dorothy wasn't guilty, perhaps we might even find something to make him less obsessed with the idea.

Mr Buttons eagerly rushed ahead of me and threw the doors to the shed open. I considered that Dorothy definitely wouldn't have left them unlocked if she was hiding evidence inside, but before I could bring it up, Mr Buttons let out a blood-curdling scream. I sprinted to catch up as fast as I could, my heart pounding. "What is it? What's wrong, Mr Buttons?"

"It's such an unseemly mess!" The colour drained from his face. "Sibyl, surely this is proof enough," he said, turning to face me and motioning to the mess in the shed. "No innocent person could keep a shed this messy!"

While I knew this was just Mr Buttons being his usual self, I couldn't help but agree on some level. The shed was in complete tatters. It was extremely dusty, which implied that it went largely unused, though I knew that couldn't be the case. It smelt of damp plants and mouldy wood, a kind of pungent mix that was entirely unpleasant.

The worst part was simply the clutter. Ancient tools and rubbish were scattered about seemingly at random, leaving almost no room to so much as move through the shed unhindered. I noticed that Mr Buttons had knelt down and was starting to tidy things up. I didn't know what else I had expected.

"Mr Buttons, we don't have time for this," I said, nearly tripping over a rake as I stepped towards him. "Dorothy could be back any minute and we don't want to be in here when she does."

Mr Buttons sighed, carefully placing a shovel neatly under a nearby table. "Very well. I'll just have to try to endure it all." He looked around the shed nervously as he spoke, clearly uncomfortable with the mess.

I grabbed Mr Buttons' arm as a scratching sound came from the door. My heart sank and I froze all over. Was that Dorothy? What was she doing? Mr Buttons and I swung around, and I saw that the door was still shut. I remained still, listening for any other sounds. After what felt like an eternity, a loud meow sounded out from the door. I breathed a massive sigh of relief, not realising exactly how nervous I had been until that moment.

"Go away, Lord Farringdon!" Mr Buttons yelled. Lord Farringdon meowed angrily in response and continued to scratch at the door. "Sibyl, he's just attracting attention! We need to get him out of here."

I nodded in agreement, but knew that no matter where we would put Lord Farringdon, he would find a way back. I made my way through the sea of junk to the shed door and opened it wide, ushering the cat quickly inside. Lord

Farringdon slowly trotted in and calmly sat down as soon as he was through the doorway. I closed the door quickly, trying to be as quiet as I could about it.

"Come on little buddy," I said softly as I leant down to pick him up. Just before I could grab him, Lord Farringdon took off, meowing wildly. He knocked things over left and right, all the time meowing loudly as he jumped all over the shed. Mr Buttons wildly flailed at him in a futile attempt to stop the cat, but ended up causing more of a ruckus.

Before I could make a move to stop him, I heard another sound that made the blood in my veins freeze. Footsteps were coming up the path, slowly but surely. "Mr Buttons!" I hissed as quietly as I could, and his expression told me that he'd heard it too. Lord Farringdon was still trying his best to destroy everything inside the shed, but it was far too late to stop him now. "Hide," I whispered, looking around desperately for a good spot as the footsteps drew nearer.

There was absolutely nowhere to hide. The shed was messy, but it was still very small. There was simply nowhere for either of us to hide, unless we could somehow flatten ourselves and hide under all of the junk. The door flung open before I could make a decision.

"What are you doing in here?" the voice demanded.

I swallowed nervously and looked up to see Cressida. I was so relieved I nearly passed out on the spot.

"We're looking for evidence that Dorothy is the murderer," Mr Buttons explained tactlessly. "She's not gone long, so we have to hurry."

"But Dorothy can't be the murderer," Cressida said simply with a small shrug. "It doesn't add up."

"We won't be long," I promised, then spoke just quietly enough for Cressida to hear, but not Mr Buttons. "It'll help him get over it."

Cressida nodded slowly. "All right, let's have a quick look. But just a quick one. I can't imagine Dorothy will be gone for long."

Lord Farringdon had stopped his outburst when Cressida entered, much to my relief. We searched through the rubbish and clutter. I was searching more slowly than I would have liked, but I had to be careful not to cut myself on anything.

"Aha!" Mr Buttons yelled triumphantly. I spun

around to see him holding a bottle of antifreeze aloft, as if it were some kind of grand trophy. "Proof!"

"Everybody has antifreeze, Mr Buttons," Cressida said flatly. "I would be more worried if she didn't have antifreeze, since it belongs in the shed and it would be more suspicious if she'd gotten rid of it. Moreover, do you know what happens to a car if it's driven without antifreeze in this weather?" she asked quite seriously, only to be met with a look of total confusion from Mr Buttons. "Let me tell you. First, the engine will overheat extremely quickly. The seals and gaskets will give out, which will cause fluid to leak into and out of places they ought not to be, which can stop parts of the engine from working altogether. Depending on how long this goes on, the entire engine might need to be scrapped. Does that sound sensible to you?" Cressida punctuated her question by putting her hands on her hips.

"We should hurry up and get out of here," I suggested. "You found the antifreeze, Mr Buttons, so it's time to go. We've been in here far too long as it is. We should put everything back the way it was." I eyed off all the damage that Lord

Farringdon had managed to inflict in his short, chaotic adventure.

Mr Buttons was silent for a moment, scratching his chin. "Yes, I suppose you're right, Sibyl. I'm not at all convinced that Dorothy's innocent, and I'm sure there's another clue in here somewhere, but we've simply spent too much time."

We furiously spent the next several minutes throwing everything back to how it was, to the best of our memory. It was practically impossible to remember the exact positioning of all the mess, but we did the best we could. Besides, I doubted that Dorothy herself could remember the position of everything, given how chaotic the shed had been.

We all started on our way back to the kitchen. I slowed my breathing in an attempt to calm down, having felt quite nervous during our little expedition. I was a bit annoyed that it was so fruitless, though I hadn't expected anything else. Mr Buttons disliked Dorothy, and while I certainly agreed that she made herself hard to like, it seemed to me that Mr Buttons was trying very hard to pin the murder on her. As we got to the kitchen door, it swung open, and an angrier-than-usual looking Dorothy blocked our path.

"What were you all doing out there?" she demanded, her accusatory tone not lost on any of us.

"Cressida *does* own this house, Dorothy, after all. You're in no position to question her movements on her own estate," Mr Buttons said in an angry tone.

"The shed is my responsibility," Dorothy said, her voice trembling slightly. "None of you, Cressida included, have any reason or business being in there, much less snooping around."

"We weren't snooping, Dorothy. Why are you so suspicious of us? Have you something to hide?" Mr Buttons asked, clearly provoking her.

"Hold on," I said, desperate to intervene. "This is ridiculous. You two are at each other's throats so often that I'm surprised you're both still standing. Can you just kiss and make up?"

Dorothy looked shocked, but Mr Buttons looked as though he were ready to throw up and run away. He took several steps back. "K...kiss?" he stammered, wild eyed. "Oh, no! Why would you suggest that, Sibyl?"

"That's disgusting," Dorothy agreed, and I suspected it was the first and last time they'd agree on anything. I sighed audibly.

"Can you at least shake hands?"

"No!" they yelled in unison.

CHAPTER 17

"Are you sure it's a good idea, Cressida?" I asked, concerned that she was making a mistake. I appreciated that she was trying to do a good thing, but it seemed to me that it could backfire all too easily. Catastrophically, even.

In light of recent events, Cressida thought it would be a good idea to invite Mortimer over for dinner with herself, Mr Buttons, and me. She opted not to invite Sally or Florence to avoid an unfortunate incident like the last time. Plus, Florence was refusing to leave the boarding house, so simply avoiding her was apparently the best approach. The dinner seemed like a good idea, but I was worried about something in particular.

"Do you think Dorothy is willing to cook? Or even able?" I asked.

Cressida smiled at me knowingly. "I'm not even willing to risk asking her. Ever since the police came to take her for questioning, she's been in a frightful mood, though I'm not sure if I can blame her. But no, Sibyl, I don't plan to ask Dorothy to cook."

My eyes widened. What was she planning? Did she have another cook already? Surely she wasn't going to cook, unless... "Wait, Cressida, you're not going to ask *me* to cook, are you?" I asked, feeling a deep sense of dread. I didn't mind cooking for close friends, but I couldn't imagine what Dorothy would do if she found me working in the kitchen.

"No, no," Cressida assured me, much to my relief. "I've given Dorothy the night off and told her that I'm going to buy take out."

"Oh," I said simply, feeling more than a little stunned at the revelation. That didn't seem at all like something Cressida would do. "That doesn't seem like you, Cressida, if I'm honest."

"Oh, no, dear," she replied with a smile. "I'll disguise it as my own cooking, of course. And you'll help me!" she declared, still smiling.

I sighed, knowing there was no real way to escape her strange scheme. "How long do we have?" I asked, trying my best not to sound like I was dreading the entire night. At least the food would be good, I figured, but it was hard to believe we could disguise anything as our own cooking.

"We have about two hours before everybody is due to arrive. That's plenty of time to order something and disguise it nicely. I'm thinking we should order pizza," Cressida suggested happily.

"Cressida, I think we should get something that's a little less, well, a little less obviously take out," I suggested, trying my best to let her down gently. "If we're going to disguise it as home cooking then we ought to get something that people are likely to cook for guests. Pizza's fine, but I think it would be a bit too obviously store bought."

Cressida considered this for several seconds before slowly nodding. "Okay, that makes sense. Thai food?" she asked, which made me realise that I was now practically in charge of this entire operation.

"Yes, that sounds fine," I said with another sigh. I don't know how she always dragged me into these strange things, but I'd rather have that than have Cressida trying to accomplish weird things all on her lonesome. We looked up the menu of a local Thai place and immediately shared a confused glance.

It was the only Thai place that was open and delivering, but the menu barely had a word of English on it. Short of words like 'Entrees,' 'Mains,' and 'Drinks,' the rest of the menu was entirely comprised of names of unpronounceable dishes. None of them had any semblance of a description, and all we could figure out was what kind of dish they were based on where they sat in the menu and their price.

While I was busy thinking of another restaurant to try, Cressida decided she'd be a bit more adventurous and called them, ordering a huge amount of food, seemingly at random. Cressida had to repeat herself over and over again as she failed to pronounce the names of dishes, so it was likely we wouldn't even receive whatever it was she was trying to order. This flimsy plan was getting even less stable by the second.

"Oh, dear," Cressida said as she hung up the phone. "Do you think Mortimer will like Thai food?"

"I have no idea," I admitted. "But I think you ordered enough to cover anybody's tastes, even if we're not sure exactly what's going to be delivered."

Cressida looked strangely relieved, which made me consider that she had a very different grasp on the situation than I did.

"Hello, you two," Mr Buttons said, announcing his arrival. "I thought I'd swing by early, seeing as I do live here and don't have much else to do."

"Mr Buttons! No!" Cressida yelled, clearly trying to hide the fact that we were ordering take out.

Mr Buttons was understandably stunned at her outcry. "Was I not invited?" he asked with no small amount of confusion.

"No, it's fine." I smiled. "Cressida's just very stressed out, since she's too scared to ask Dorothy to cook, given the mood Dorothy's in."

"Oh, I see," Mr Buttons said with a nod. "What's the plan, then? Are you cooking for us, Cressida?"

"Yes! No!" she yelled, clearly flustered.

"We both are," I lied, hoping to give her some time to calm down and think rationally. Then again, I wasn't sure Cressida was much for rational thinking, regardless of how calm she felt. "But I'm afraid we're very busy, so we'll have to ask you to come back when dinner's ready."

"Oh, of course," Mr Buttons said. "I wouldn't want to interrupt. Well, good day, ladies. I'll see you this evening." He walked away as Cressida managed to catch her breath.

"Cressida, I'm not going to lie. I'm losing confidence in your ability to keep up this charade," I admitted, turning to face her. "Dinner hasn't actually arrived yet and you've nearly blown our story."

"I know, I know," she said sadly. "He just took me by surprise. I'll be fine! I promise."

Cressida and I sat around for several more minutes, discussing exactly how we planned to disguise our food as home cooking. We decided that it should be fairly easy to get away with since nobody would expect us to be doing this. Besides, I hardly believed that we were doing it either. On top of that, we only needed to fool Mr Buttons and Mortimer. Mr Buttons never ordered take out, and Mortimer was from out of town, so there was no chance that either of them would be familiar with the food.

Eventually the food arrived. Cressida ran to the door to answer while I staged the kitchen to look as if we'd been cooking, as was the plan. We still had a little while until everybody was going to arrive, which meant we would need to keep the food warm anyway. I wasn't crazy about the idea of using the kitchen when Dorothy was around, but with Cressida helping me, it wasn't quite so bad. I couldn't imagine even Dorothy would be too upset, considering that it was her boss who was using the kitchen. Then again, this was Dorothy, so who really knew?

Cressida eventually came back cradling a rather large amount of food. I don't know how she was managing to carry it all, but she deposited it on top of the countertop without asking for help.

"How much did you buy?" I asked, my mouth hanging open. The food was piled up high, and I suspected that if we were to pile it straight up it would easily reach the ceiling.

"Hang on, I have to get the other half," Cressida said, breathing heavily. She wandered back to the front door, leaving me in shock. I decided that it was best just to start the plan, since time was of the essence. Cressida could always ask if she needed help carrying the rest.

She came back with another equally large pile of food as I was busy stirring some kind of delicious meat, vegetable, and noodle dish in a large pot. I was trying to make it look as messy as possible so that everybody would assume we had cooked it from scratch.

We spent the next several minutes 'cooking' the food, keeping it warm, and ruining all the effort that the poor take out cooks had put into making the food look pristine. Eventually it was time, and Cressida went out to wait for Mortimer. I stayed back and started to dish up the food, wondering how on earth Cressida had managed to carry it all in just two trips. There was enough to feed a small army, and it seemed like we wouldn't be able to eat it all no matter how hard we tried. Though, try we would, as the food smelt and looked absolutely delicious.

I took some bowls and plates out into the dining room to see that everybody had already arrived and was seated. Mr Buttons smiled warmly, and Mortimer stood up to greet me.

"Hello, Sibyl," he said, his expression as

neutral as ever. "Cressida was just telling us about all the hard work you've put into cooking this afternoon. I must say, it smells wonderful."

"Oh, uh, yes," I stammered awkwardly, trying to place the food on the table. "Yes, thank you. Cressida did a fair bit of it herself, actually."

"Oh, I see," he said, smiling at Cressida. "And what's this dish called?" he asked, pointing to a kind of yellow rice dish in the centre of the table.

Cressida was shocked into stunned silence, so I cleared my throat and thought of a response. "Oh, uh, cow...mockay," I replied, hoping he'd buy my bluff and not realise it was simply random gibberish.

"Oh, it's Khao Mok Kai? That's one of my favourites." Mortimer took a seat as he spoke, looking at the food eagerly.

Cressida and I sighed audibly with relief. We brought out the rest of the food and dished it up for everybody, finally sitting down to eat for ourselves. It was a huge relief, knowing that Mortimer was unlikely to question the food any further. More than that, all the worry and work had made me hungry, so I ate the food ravenously. It was delicious, too, all kinds of spices, meats, vegetables, and types of rice combined into amazing flavours. The more I ate, the more I found it hard to believe that anybody would believe that Cressida and I had cooked it.

We ate in relative silence, everybody clearly enjoying the meal. Mr Buttons and Mortimer made the occasional comment on how delicious the food was, to which Cressida and I responded with awkward thanks before quickly changing the subject.

Mortimer was sitting directly next to Cressida, and it was clear to everybody except perhaps to Mortimer himself that they were flirting. Then again, he was simply impossible to read, so maybe he knew full well what was happening.

It was also astoundingly obvious to me that Mr Buttons was none too happy about the situation. He constantly shot glances at Mortimer and Cressida as they spoke, looking less than pleased with how their friendship was developing. Other than Mr Buttons' obvious discomfort, the dinner went very well. Nobody questioned that we'd managed to cook the meal, and Mr Buttons seemed to enjoy himself in the end, despite some obvious jealousy. I wondered what Cressida and

Mortimer would be like as a couple, but it was hard to imagine Mortimer expressing himself much at all, unless it was over one of Cressida's horrifying paintings.

CHAPTER 18

Waves of guilt washed over me as I looked around the café. It was quite a trendy café, a new one in Pharmidale and sufficiently out of the way—or so I hoped—that the detectives would not see me sitting there with Blake.

He was over at the counter, ordering our coffees and lunch, while I was sitting at a table surveying the surroundings. The aroma of the coffee was pungent and welcoming. Some of the furniture had been made from recycled industrial items, items I did not recognise, but it added to the effect. Numerous clear light fittings hung from the ceilings, lighted rather spectacularly by spiral Edison filaments.

"I was surprised when you invited me. Are you sure this is a good idea?" I asked Blake when he returned to the table.

He shot me a blank look. "I'm not sure what you mean."

I gestured to the both of us. "You know, us. The detectives don't want us dating."

Blake arched his eyebrows. "That's why I suggested lunch rather than dinner."

I could not help but laugh. "Isn't that splitting hairs?"

Blake shrugged. "I'm willing to take the risk. After all, they did find Dorothy's DNA on the envelope, so that gives them all the more reason to suspect her rather than you."

I was surprised. "You don't think Dorothy did it, do you?"

Blake shrugged again. "I know it wasn't you, or Mr Buttons or Cressida. That leaves Dorothy, Sally Cavendish, Prudence Paget, or someone else that we don't know about. The most simple solution is usually the answer. It has to be one of those three, in my book."

I nodded. "Yes, although I can't see what motive Dorothy could possibly have. Roland hadn't even insulted her cooking, because he had that genetic disorder where people can't taste food. So surely that would've had to make him the person least likely to be murdered by Dorothy. Prudence, on the other hand, had a motive, because Roland had refused her grant years ago, and Sally had a motive, because he had a mistress, that awful woman Florence. Although I did see Sally with a man that day, so perhaps she has a lover of her own."

I stopped speaking when the waitress placed our coffees in front of us. When she was out of earshot, Blake spoke. "I've just found out the man's identity, only this morning. He's an old friend of Roland and Sally's, a local minister at the Uniting Church. Sally has been friends with him and his wife for years."

"So there's no chance that they were having an affair?"

Blake put two packets of sugar into his coffee before stirring it. "Definitely no affair there. I'm certain of it."

"Well, that makes Sally unlikely to be a suspect then, given she was so upset when she met his mistress."

Blake took a sip of his coffee before answering. "To the contrary, it does give her a motive.

Many women have murdered their husbands for the very same reason."

"But she seemed to be in love with him," I protested.

"There's a fine line between love and hate."

Our meals arrived, and I ate mine, considering that this was a far happier time than our dinner of the previous night. Things were looking up. Blake was determined to date me despite the detectives' wishes, and even they now had another suspect, Dorothy. I looked up to see Blake staring intently at me.

"Sibyl, you said your settlement is nearly through?"

I nodded. "Yes, as I told you, it's been awarded, so I'm just waiting for the money to arrive in my bank."

"What will you do then?"

"I don't really know," I said. "For a start, I'll stop stressing about money and the future." I smiled as a cloud of happiness settled over me.

"Will you stay in Little Tatterford?"

Blake's question took me by surprise. "Yes, of course I will. This is my home now. I have friends here. I've made a life here."

"I thought you might think of moving back to the city."

"Sydney? No, that hasn't even crossed my mind." My stomach fluttered wildly when I saw the palpable look of relief pass across Blake's face.

Blake opened his mouth, and I was sure he was about to say something romantic, when there was a loud crash. I jumped and spun around in my seat to see that a small child had dropped a glass of some sort of drink on the floor. The child immediately burst into loud tears, while her mother tried to comfort her. The waitress ran out and tried to assure both mother and child that it was all fine, to no avail.

I turned back, right as my text tone signalled an incoming text. It was from Mr Buttons.

The phone was closer to Blake than it was to me, and I saw him looking at it, and as he did, he frowned. I picked up the phone and read the text.

We're booked in tomorrow. Prison. James. I've booked our tickets to Brisbane.

Blake was the first to speak. "Sorry I saw that message, Sibyl."

I waved his apologies away, but he continued. "Sibyl, I'm concerned that you and Mr Buttons are investigating. I'm concerned for your safety."

I ran my fingers through my hair, and then jumped as the child emitted a particularly loud, high pitched shriek. "I'm only doing it to make Mr Buttons happy," I said. "You know how he's firmly convinced that Dorothy did it. He's sure that James, given that he's Dorothy's nephew, will have some dirt on Dorothy."

Blake shook his head. "Sibyl, *someone* was the murderer. If that person thinks you're getting too close, then you could be in danger."

"No one knows we're going to visit James," I said, "least of all the detectives, as they told me not to leave town. I seriously *am* only doing it to keep Mr Buttons happy. The thing is, he said it would take ages for the paperwork to visit James to be processed, so I can't understand how we're getting in so soon."

"That's because it won't be a personal visit," Blake said.

"What do you mean?"

"It takes a long time for the paperwork to be processed when you want to visit an inmate in person, with no barriers between you," Blake explained. "You'll have to speak to him tomorrow through a glass barrier. It's called a non contact visit. I'm sure you've seen that on TV."

I agreed that I had. "So do you mean that the paperwork is only for a visit with no barriers?" I asked him. "And it's much easier and faster to arrange to visit a prisoner if you speak to them behind a wall?"

"That's right. You have to be there an hour before your appointment time, in order to be processed," Blake said. "If you're not there an hour beforehand, they won't let you in, no matter what. Anyway, I don't know why I'm helping you, because I don't want you to go."

I squirmed uncomfortably in my seat. Just then, my phone rang. The Caller ID showed that it was Mr Buttons—what bad timing! I wasn't going to answer, but Blake indicated that I should. "Hi, Mr Buttons. I'm here with Blake," I said by way of answer.

Mr Buttons disregarded my warning, and launched into a spiel about the prison visit the following day. I finished the conversation as fast as I could, only too aware of Blake's opinion about the matter. I switched off my phone and put it in my handbag.

Blake reached across the table and took my hand in his. "Sibyl, please stay safe."

CHAPTER 19

The plane ride had been turbulent, and we had to keep our seatbelts on for most of the flight. Even worse, the coffee had been disgusting, almost undrinkable. Added to my dismay was the fact that I was only coming with Mr Buttons to keep him happy. I'd had to cancel several of my appointments to make the trip to Brisbane, and the fact that it was going to be a wasted day was irritating me somewhat. Still, I told myself to make the most of it.

"That was the worst flight ever!" I clutched my stomach.

Mr Buttons continued to look out the window of the prisoner transport bus. His next statement showed that he had ignored my comment. "I don't know why they call this a prisoner transport bus, when it's transporting visitors of prisoners, not the prisoners themselves."

I shrugged. There was no point complaining about the plane ride to Mr Buttons. He was entirely too consumed with excitement, as he was so utterly convinced that he would discover Dorothy's motive for murdering Roland Cavendish. It was impossible to convince him that she hadn't even known the man, apart from his short stay at the boarding house.

I was relieved when we finally approached our destination. It was a stereotypical prison, just what I had imagined, grey concrete, grey iron, and everywhere I looked there were high steel fences. In fact, everywhere I looked there were five layers of coiled barbed wire. The green lawns beside the dark grey tarmac road did not provide any relief. I was hugely intimidated.

We followed the signs to the front office, where the people in front of us ripped a ticket from a ticket machine and then walked through a security gate. Mr Buttons and I did likewise.

A guard appeared and directed first time visitors to form a line at the side. I was at once taken into a separate room. A rather scary looking prison officer took my ID and spent some time tapping into a computer. He then informed me that he was going to fingerprint me by using the Biometric Identification System.

"Fingerprint me?" I said, alarmed. "I thought only criminals were fingerprinted."

The man shook his head. "This is not a fingerprint image as such. It scans the finger to create a mathematical template. It cannot be matched against fingerprint images. It's stored in our computer database, along with your photo, details of your identification, name, address and date of birth." I was still puzzled, but the man continued. "It's simply to make the visitor system easier, and to hasten the time it takes visitors to be processed."

I nodded, although being 'processed' wasn't a term with which I felt too comfortable.

After the man took great pains over my identification documents, and fingerprinted me, he told me I would later have to put all personal items in a locker: my handbag, my paperwork, my jewellery and any hair ties and a belt. I wasn't wearing a belt or a hair tie, but I supposed he gave the same speech to everyone.

After about half an hour, he directed me to

join the other first time visitors in the waiting room. Mr Buttons was already waiting for me. There were several other people within earshot, so I leant forward to Mr Buttons and whispered, "Why are you wearing that red armband?"

Mr Buttons shrugged. "They told me that all male visitors are issued with red armbands, and that it's not to be removed under any circumstances."

"I see. I suppose that's in case some prisoners escape, as it's their way of being able to tell you apart from the prisoners."

Mr Buttons looked alarmed. "Is that supposed to reassure me, Sibyl?"

Mr Buttons and I sat in the waiting room for around half an hour, barely speaking to each other. There was nothing really to say, and I was a little nervous about meeting James. After all, the last time I had seen James, he had tried to throw me out a window to my death. Actually, that was the second last time I had seen him. The last time was when I had given evidence against him in court. I'm sure I wasn't his favourite person.

I looked around the room, but could find nothing of any interest on which to focus. It was the same prison grey, albeit a darker shade. The walls were grey, and the cold hard plastic chairs were grey. The room smelt of disinfectant, something akin to the smell of a hospital. Finally, a guard appeared and announced that he would take us all to another building to have our non contact visit with the prisoners.

I was surprised to see that Mr Buttons was shaking, whether it was from nerves or anticipation that in his belief that he would finally get evidence against Dorothy, was anyone's guess.

It was quite a walk to the other building, a walk along a concrete pathway flanked by tall steel fences. It reminded me of the list they had given us of items we were not allowed to bring into the prison, items such as explosives, weapons, and ladders as well as grappling hooks. I bit back a smile. I wondered if any visitors had ever attempted to bring in such items.

We arrived at yet another grey concrete building, and were given a locker key. We were instructed to put absolutely everything in the lockers, including the entire contents of our pockets, even any tissues. After everyone put their stuff in the lockers, we were given a name tag to wear around our neck.

A burly prison guard appeared. "Everyone

here for the ten o-clock appointment, line up on the yellow line!" he barked. He reminded me of an army drill sergeant, not that I had ever seen one in person.

After we lined up on the yellow line, a dog on a leash appeared. The guard announced that this was a drug dog, and we were not to touch him. The dog made his way up and down the line, sniffing. I felt guilty, and even more intimidated. It was an awful experience, and I fervently wished I had never agreed to come. I hoped Mr Buttons would not feel the inclination to straighten the dog's collar, or any such thing.

To my relief, we all passed the dog's inspection, and were ushered into a corridor. One by one, we had our fingerprints scanned. My photo popped up on the screen, along with the word 'Accepted.' I breathed a sigh of relief. I returned to the line and waited until everyone had been fingerprinted.

We were then told to take off our shoes, and our shoes were passed through a metal detector. After that, we all had to walk through a metal detector, and then turn out our pockets. I just wanted to turn and run.

"People for contact visits stand over here, and

people for non contact visits stand over there," a guard yelled. After Mr Buttons and I lined up with about a quarter of the people present, we were all given a number, and then we were ushered in like cattle to our assigned seats. To my surprise, there was absolutely no privacy. Mr Buttons and I were shoulder to shoulder with strangers.

I sat down on a dark blue, hard, uncomfortable plastic chair. "Where are the prisoners?" I asked Mr Buttons.

"I suppose they'll come in next," he said.

There were rows and rows of glass booths. I had expected a phone, but the glass had mesh at the bottom, so we were obviously to speak through that. Once again, we had to wait, although the wait this time was about five minutes. All at once came the loud sound of yelling and laughter, and footsteps. "That must be the prisoners coming," Mr Buttons said.

The prisoners entered the room on the other side of the glass booths, all together. I shuddered when I saw James. I was sure it was all a bad idea.

"What are you doing here?" James said without preamble. "I didn't think I'd ever see either of you again. Do you realise that I have to wait in the holding room for one hour before I have visitors and for one hour after?"

I stuttered out an apology, and would have said more, but James kept speaking. "And I'm only allowed to have two visitors a week, so now I won't be allowed to have any more for a whole week." He pouted, but in a mean way.

I figured that prison had only hardened him. His soft, sulky face had been replaced with hard lines. Mr Buttons interrupted my thoughts. "Do you get many visitors?"

James leant back and laughed. "No. The only visitor I get is Frank."

"Frank?" I echoed. "Oh that's right, Dorothy's son. Your cousin." Frank used to visit Dorothy at the boarding house, but I hadn't seen him in ages. I felt sorry for him, as Dorothy was even meaner to him than she was to the boarding house guests.

James shrugged. "He rarely visits, and Herman hasn't even visited me once."

"Herman?" Mr Buttons and I spoke in unison. "Who's he?" I asked.

"Frank's brother," James spat. "Anyway, what are you two doing here?"

Mr Buttons came straight to the point.

"Dorothy. We've come about Dorothy. I assume you don't like her?'

James looked interested. "I can't stand the old bat. She was the one who put me in to the cops. I've never liked her. And poor Frank! She's been so mean to him. She's a bully! Herman was her favourite son." His speech disintegrated into a verbal tirade against Dorothy.

Mr Buttons looked entirely too pleased. "I am quite sure that Dorothy has murdered a boarding house guest, but the police have been unable to connect her to the victim. I wondered if you had any idea."

James shrugged, but his eyes sparkled with interest. "Who was the victim?"

"Roland Cavendish."

James burst into laughter. "You're kidding! Cavendish the quantum physicist? Well, sure, Dorothy killed him."

I felt my jaw drop open. I just couldn't take it in. Was James joking? But how would he know that Roland had been a quantum physicist? What was going on? I looked at Mr Buttons, but he was rubbing his hands together with undisguised glee.

"Did Dorothy know Roland?" he asked.

James hesitated, and I could clearly see he was

having an inner struggle. He did not want to help us, but he despised Dorothy. Finally, he decided to speak. "Dorothy's son, Herman, was her favourite son, or to be precise, the only son she liked. She always said he was the only one in the family who had any brains. She was always horrible to Frank—always said he was a good-for-nothing and that he'd never amount to anything. She'd buy Herman new clothes, designer brands, and she'd buy Frank's clothes from the thrift store. I'm not kidding. Anyway, Herman was doing a doctoral thesis in quantum physics, and Roland Cavendish was his supervisor. He failed Herman's Ph.D."

I butted in. "But supervisors can't fail Ph.D.'s."

James shook his head. "I don't remember all the details, but Cavendish sent the thesis to some obscure examiners who had the opposite point of view to Herman. He set Herman up to fail. Anyway, Herman was disgraced in academia and left to travel the world backpacking, leaving Dorothy to work as a cook. Prior to that, Herman had been on good pay, and Dorothy didn't have to work. After his Ph.D. was failed, he turned to gambling and alcohol. Dorothy found out that Cavendish published Herman's work as his own."

I was shocked throughout the whole revelation. "But how?" I asked. "How did Roland get away with it? Didn't Herman complain?"

James shook his head. "Herman was a stuck up pig, but he went into rehab in northern India. Cavendish published Herman's work when Herman was in rehab."

"But didn't Herman complain when he got out of rehab?" Mr Buttons asked.

James snorted rudely. "No, because when he got out of rehab, he went to Tibet and became a Tibetan Buddhist. Then he met a girl from Kyrgyzstan who looks like you, Sibyl, come to think of it. Frank told me all that. Anyway, the nerve of that old bat! She accused *me* of murder and then she went and killed Cavendish!"

The rest of the meeting was a blur, although we left soon after James's disclosure. All I remembered after that was Mr Buttons' mantra of, 'I told you so! I told you so!' as we collected our things from the lockers and went back on the transport bus for the flight home, a flight where all I heard was Mr Buttons saying, "I told you so! I told you so!"

CHAPTER 20

I was still in disbelief. I was having trouble accepting the fact that Dorothy had a motive. Could Mr Buttons indeed have been right, after all?

We had called Blake from the prisoner transport bus and told him what we'd learned. When I turned my phone back on after the flight, he hadn't called me, and I didn't like to call him again while he was working. All I could do was wait it out.

Mr Buttons, on the other hand, was most anxious to find out if Dorothy had been arrested for the murder of Roland Cavendish. I had pointed out to him that we had only discovered that Dorothy had a motive, and that we already knew full well that Prudence Paget had a motive, but that, of course, had fallen on deaf ears.

We had called Cressida several times, but she hadn't answered. I secretly hoped that Dorothy wasn't holding her hostage, or worse. Of course, I didn't voice those concerns to Mr Buttons. He was already nervous enough.

When the taxi arrived at the boarding house, I saw with great relief that Cressida was standing at the end of the path. Mr Buttons paid the driver, while I hurried over to Cressida. "Mr Buttons and I called and called you! I thought something had happened to you! Why didn't you answer your phone?" I pulled my jacket tightly around me as the cold assaulted me.

Cressida pulled her phone from her pocket. "Oh, I didn't hear it. It says I've had missed calls." She handed the phone to me and I saw that it was set to silent. I explained this, fixed it, and handed it back to her.

Mr Buttons hurried up behind me. "What's happening about Dorothy? Has she been arrested?"

Cressida shook her head. "I can't believe it! I just can't believe it." She dabbed at her eyes furiously, and it was only then that I noticed some black pools of mascara beneath her eyes.

"Can't believe what?" Mr Buttons said altogether too sharply.

"Dorothy, of course."

I could see Mr Buttons growing impatient, so I hurried to speak. "Cressida, we've had a long flight. In fact, we had two long flights, and a horrible experience visiting someone in a maximum security prison. Could you please tell us exactly what has happened with Dorothy, and tell us fast."

Cressida clutched her throat. "The detectives came here, wanting to question Dorothy."

"And?" I prompted.

"They didn't arrest her."

"What?" Mr Buttons shrieked.

Cressida shook her head. "She did a runner."

I was silent for a moment while I tried to process that information. "What do you mean, exactly?"

Cressida gestured expansively around herself. "She was in the kitchen when the detectives arrived, and I'd finally convinced that awful woman, Florence, to leave the boarding house, so I was checking her out. I pointed the detectives in the direction of the kitchen, and then they came back. They were quite upset, and they said that there was no sign of Dorothy." She sniffled again for a few moments before continuing. "They said they wanted to question Dorothy over the murder of Roland."

"Get a grip on yourself, madam," Mr Buttons said kindly. "It will all be all right. Where is Dorothy now?"

Cressida shrugged. "That's just it. No one knows. I called and called her at the top of my lungs, and the detectives searched the house, but there's no sign of her. One minute she was there, and the next minute she had vanished. She even left food bubbling away on the stove, and it's not like her to do something so irresponsible."

Mr Buttons and I exchanged glances. "Proof that she's guilty all right," he said. "She's trying to flee from justice."

"All her clothes are still in her room," Cressida said. "Those detectives are waiting inside the house for her to return."

"I didn't see their car," I said.

"She's hardly likely to return if the detectives' car is parked outside the boarding house. Detective Roberts drove away and Blake brought him back, and then Blake himself drove away," Cressida said. She patted Mr Buttons' arm. "Mr Buttons, I do believe you were right about Dorothy all along."

Mr Buttons beamed, and I rubbed my temples. All I wanted was to have a glass of wine, two Advil, and a good night's sleep. I had a suspicion that it wasn't going to happen. "And did Blake speak to you?" I asked Cressida.

She shook her head. "I overheard the detectives speaking to him. They sent him to Dorothy's son Frank's house to see if she was there."

Mr Buttons turned to me. "What are we going to do?"

I let out a long sigh. "There's nothing we can do, really. I'm going home to have a shower and a glass of wine. I'm exhausted after today. Anyway, I have to light my fire in a hurry before my cottage turns into a giant icicle."

Mr Buttons shook his head. "No, I don't think it's safe. Dorothy could be lying in wait for you there."

I winced. "What? You don't think she wants to murder me, too?"

Cressida intervened. "Mr Buttons, of course Dorothy doesn't want to hurt Sibyl."

"She *did* try to set her up to take the fall for the murder," Mr Buttons said, his teeth chattering from the cold. "She murdered Roland in Sibyl's cottage."

"We don't even know if she *is* the murderer yet," I said, "not for sure."

Mr Buttons shook his head. "Sibyl, it's as plain as the nose on your face. Dorothy is indeed the murderer. Why else would she make a run for it when the police came looking for her?"

I had to admit that he had a point.

"Why don't you come inside and have some dinner here?" Cressida asked me. "You can't go back to your cottage. Haven't you seen all those movies where the person goes back to her house, thinking she's safe, only to encounter the murderer who is waiting for her in the dark, about to slit her throat?"

I clutched at my neck. "What a way to put it, Cressida!" I imagined myself in one of her upcoming paintings, and shuddered. "Look, I'm sure Dorothy doesn't have anything against me, not personally. My shower and a glass of wine are calling me. I bought an expensive bottle of wine to celebrate the property settlement being awarded to me. I was going to share it with all of you, but after the day I've had…" My voice trailed away.

Mr Buttons puffed out his chest. "You can drink wine at another time, honestly. The woman is crazed! She's on a mission to kill, don't you understand? I have no more patience for the silly antics of that woman."

"What I understand, Mr Buttons, is that I have a new bottle of expensive wine."

"If you truly insist on going, Sibyl, I will just have to accompany you. I wouldn't be a gentleman if I didn't."

"Oh very crafty, Mr Buttons. You just want a glass of that wine."

Mr Buttons chuckled. "You found me out. You can't keep an old dog down. Goodbye, Cressida, please stay close to the detectives and keep an eye out for Dorothy. Go inside and get warm."

I walked down the road with Mr Buttons hot on my heels. "You know," I said to Mr Buttons, "I've never seen you so happy, now that it seems that Dorothy did it. I know you've always disliked her, but I didn't really mind her too much."

Mr Buttons scoffed and came to a stop right by the old rusty water tank that loomed precariously above us. "Don't be ridiculous, Sibyl! I didn't dislike her! I hated her. She's a mean old cow. No, that's too kind—she's a hideous hag of a wench who insisted that everyone eat her greasy, grimy, good-for-nothing horrendous food."

I was shocked at Mr Buttons' vehemence. He paused his tirade to pull a pebble out of his shoe, and he flung it at the water tank. It made a clanging sound that reverberated into the cold night air. We made to walk off when Mr Buttons started up again. "Good thing she's gone. Hopefully, Cressida will get a new cook who will serve food that doesn't taste like musty old socks."

"How dare you! My cooking is delightful!"

I spun around just as Mr Buttons clutched my arm. "Did you hear that?" he asked me.

I looked around me. "Where did the voice come from?"

"It sounds as if the old hag has died, crossed over to the other side, and now her hideous spectre is wailing."

"There's nothing wrong with my cooking, you bloated toad!" the voice screamed.

"Your chocolate mint sundae killed Roland Cavendish!" Mr Buttons yelled back.

"A pity I didn't poison you, too, you pompous old fool!"

Then it dawned on me. Dorothy was in the water tank! I couldn't get my phone out of my pocket fast enough. I called Cressida to ask her to tell the detectives that Dorothy was hiding in the old water tank near my cottage.

"Yes," Cressida said calmly. "Lord Farringdon just now told me. I was on my way to tell the detectives."

I hung up, and saw that Mr Buttons was standing directly under the water tank, looking up at it. "Mr Buttons, I wouldn't stand under that tank if I were you. It's a wonder it can take a person's weight at all. You don't want it to bottom out and have Dorothy falling on you."

Just as I said the words, there was a tearing, ripping sound, accompanied by a scream. I saw Dorothy's legs, soon followed by the rest of her, falling through the bottom of the tank as the whole bottom of the tank gave way, and Dorothy landed right on top of Mr Buttons. Both of them screamed wildly and flailed their arms.

I watched the scene unfold, dumbstruck, as the detectives sprinted down the pathway. "What do we have here?" Detective Roberts said. "This is no time for such goings-on."

His words made Mr Buttons yell even louder.

Detective Henderson pulled Dorothy off Mr Buttons, which was hard to do, as they were rolling around, their legs entwined, and Dorothy appeared to be trying to slap Mr Buttons. As Dorothy aimed a punch at his face, Henderson expertly pulled her wrists behind her back, before pulling out his handcuffs and slapping them on her wrists.

Mr Buttons staggered to his feet and rounded on Detective Roberts. "I can assure you, sir, that the dreadful murdering woman and I were certainly not involved in any type of tryst. In fact, I abhor the woman."

Roberts tried to go to the assistance of his partner, given the fact that Dorothy was struggling hard and had stomped on the detective's foot, but Mr Buttons blocked his way, and continued to give him a good dressing down.

CHAPTER 21

"Congratulations, Sibyl!" Mr Buttons said, holding up a glass of wine. Everyone cheered and did the same, clinking their glasses together before taking a drink. I smiled shyly at everybody, enjoying the attention more than I usually would.

Since Dorothy had been arrested and had confessed at length, even confessing she had left a note for Roland pretending to be from me, inviting him to my cottage for a sundae and a dalliance, we were celebrating the fact that I had been cleared of all suspicion. Mr Buttons was also celebrating the fact that Dorothy had been arrested and that he'd been right, something he wouldn't let us hear the end of for many years to come. I was sure of that.

I had invited Mr Buttons, Cressida, and, of course, Blake to my cottage. We were sitting on chairs around the fire, huddling as close as we could to the flames. While it made for a nice intimate environment, the cold was so biting that I briefly considered setting my entire cottage on fire for the warmth it would provide.

"Do you have enough wood?" Blake asked, suspiciously eyeing the fire. It hadn't occurred to me until that moment, but if the fire went out then the night would be over before it had really begun. I thought for a moment about how much wood I had left before replying.

"Yes, a little bit. It should be enough to last the night. Probably. I hope," I admitted with a sigh. "Cressida, you really need to find a new wood man. He's not delivering nearly enough, nor quickly enough. Plus, the wood's green."

Cressida looked at me with a confused expression. "But he's so nice," she said, clearly deep in thought. "And Dorothy recommended him, so he can't be all bad."

We all looked at Cressida dumbfounded for several seconds until we realised she was serious.

"Cressida," Mr Buttons said softly, "do you think perhaps that Dorothy isn't the best reference for hard working, honest people?"

It took about a full minute for Cressida to realise what Mr Buttons meant, and watching it dawn on her slowly was almost painful. "Oh," she said simply, still seeming a bit confused. "I suppose I'll look for a new wood man tomorrow, then. I still need to find a new cook," she continued, staring absent-mindedly into the fire.

"We can help you look, Cressida," I suggested. "I know there aren't too many cooks in a small town like this who are looking for work, but surely if we all pitch in we'll be able to find somebody."

"I know a few in Pharmidale," Blake piped up, managing to tear himself away from the fire to pat Cressida's shoulder. "I'm not sure if they're looking for work, but I'll ask around."

"Yes, I'll help too," Mr Buttons suggested. "I need to have a hand in choosing the new cook. After all, I'll be able to tell if they're a bad sort. And I hope people will listen to me this time," he said pointedly, eyeing us individually.

Cressida smiled, clearly relieved at the offers of help. "Thank you, everybody. Hopefully it won't take long. I do love your cucumber sandwiches, Mr Buttons, but I don't think I could sustain myself on them for long. Oh, I'll have to let Lord Farringdon help choose the new cook, too," she said, her voice trailing off again.

I felt a little bit bad for Cressida. While we all had to deal with the murders in some way—after all, I had not only been a suspect, but the murder had happened in my cottage—it was Cressida who always had to deal with the problems it caused her business afterwards.

Luckily, the press seemed to be pushing the angle that Dorothy was the long-running problem, and now that she was gone, the boarding house would be safe. Whether or not it was true wasn't even the issue, since business had been picking up since Dorothy had been arrested. Then again, maybe it had nothing to do with the murders and more to do with the fact that people just didn't want to be anywhere near the woman.

"Well, I'm glad you're off the hook, Sibyl," Blake said with a smile. "It would be hard to justify spending all this time with a murderer."

"Oh, you could have just gotten a job as a prison guard, surely," I teased, making Blake laugh.

"Shut up! You smell!" Max squawked loudly

across the room. I sighed, knowing he wasn't going to stop anytime soon. I loved Max, but I often wondered if it was possible to buy a kind of humane cockatoo muzzle. Still, I figured that the very notion of a muzzle was inhumane to an animal that loved to speak, much to my disappointment.

"I hate to say I told you so, but…" Mr Buttons began before I cut him off.

"You don't hate to say 'I told you so'! You say it all the time. You've said it about thirty times in the past hour," I berated him. I was only half joking, but Mr Buttons had made a point of telling us all that he had always known that Dorothy was a murderer. Over and over and over again.

"Ah, but it's true," he said, stroking his chin. "If you'd listened to me, we could have saved a lot of time and stress."

"You also said that Dorothy was responsible for the Vietnam War!" I all but yelled.

"I believe she may have a hand in it, yes," Mr Buttons said, turning up his nose.

"She couldn't have been too old when it began," I pleaded fruitlessly. "I know you were right about Dorothy, but I think it was more that you didn't like her than being based on any kind of logic."

Mr Buttons looked at me for a moment as he scratched his chin. "Well, it's true that I wasn't her biggest fan, so perhaps some of my accusations were slightly biased. All the same, I knew she was a bad egg. She killed Roland due to a personal grudge, but she had no excuse to involve you, Sibyl. She did her best to frame you as the murderer."

Sandy looked up at us from her bed in front of the fire, annoyed that we were talking. She plopped her head back down and fell asleep almost immediately, snoring loudly. I wondered what it would be like to be a dog: being fed for free, having the best bed in the house, and being able to demand attention from your loved ones whenever you wanted it.

Blake put his arm around me and held me tight, keeping me warm. I smiled and snuggled in closer. I might not have had the free food, but at least I had the attention.

∾

The next book in this series is:

The Last Mango in Paris

It takes two to mango, but only one to murder.

Even though Cressida's builder gives her the crepes, she's still a oui bit upset that their paths won't croissant again. In fact, she cannot beret. That's because he's been smothered with a mango, and Mr. Buttons has been found standing over the body.

But the police don't give a Notre Dame—they believe it was Mr Buttons the culprit wanted to kill!

Soon Sybil realizes this is no ordinary crime. It seems as though Mr Buttons has been Lyon about his past and baguette to mention a few secrets of his own . . .

ABOUT MORGANA BEST

USA Today Bestselling author Morgana Best survived a childhood of deadly spiders and venomous snakes in the Australian outback. Morgana Best writes cozy mysteries and enjoys thinking of delightful new ways to murder her victims.

www.morganabest.com